HER DEADLY DOUBLE LIFE

A Carolina McKay Thriller

TONY URBAN
DREW STRICKLAND

Copyright © 2020 by Packanack Publishing, Tony Urban & Drew Strickland

Visit Tony on the web: http://tonyurbanauthor.com

Visit Drew on the web: http://drewstricklandbooks.com

Cover by Jonathan Schuler: http://www.schulercreativelab.com/

All rights reserved.

No part of this book may be reproduced in any form or by any electronic or mechanical means, including information storage and retrieval systems, without written permission from the author, except for the use of brief quotations in a book review.

This is a work of fiction. Names, characters, businesses, places, events, locales, and incidents are either the products of the author's imagination or used in a fictitious manner. Any resemblance to actual persons, living or dead, or actual events is purely coincidental.

"And the crow once called the raven black."

— GEORGE R.R. MARTIN

"Birds born in a cage think flying is an illness."

— ALEJANDRO JODOROWSKY

CHAPTER ONE

The smell of pig shit hung in the humid, midsummer air as the man stepped out of his car. He snapped his hand across his mouth and nose, trying to hold it at bay, but it was too late. The odor had invaded his sinuses and would linger there for hours.

Even after all these years he wondered, why did pigs have to be the boy's damned hobby? Why couldn't he be normal and have interests outside of these disgusting creatures? Of course, *Why couldn't he be normal* was a much bigger question than anyone could answer and the man knew it.

He stared at the dark farmhouse. Even though the sun had set an hour earlier, no lights were on so the man swiveled his attention toward the barn which sat a hundred yards away.

"Earl?" the man called, his voice echoing across the flat fields. "Are you out here?"

He waited, but there was no answer.

"Asshole," the man muttered.

This was supposed to be a quick trip, dropping off some groceries. He hadn't planned on traipsing across the property, wasn't dressed for it. He slipped off his suit jacket, worried that too much time in this rancid air would contaminate it, and tossed it into the back of his Mercedes, beside the bags of TV dinners and canned goods.

Then he took a long, distraught look at his dress shoes. The Berluti's had set him back north of $1,400 and the realization that he'd have to risk destroying them in this minefield was almost enough to make him get back in the car and drive away. But that would only lead to other sorts of problems, ones for which he had little patience these days, and he trudged forward.

The barn obfuscated the moon, becoming an eerie, glowing silhouette on the otherwise barren landscape. Much of the unease he felt was the fault of the relative silence though. He could never get used to the quiet out here, in the country, where the din of traffic, of distant sirens, of civilization, took a back seat to crickets and mosquitos. The only break from the bugs were the pigs.

Those damnable pigs. Rooting, snorting, squealing. He'd been a bacon every morning type of guy before the farm came into his life. Before the pigs. When he saw up close what they were like, he'd been turned off all things pork forever.

He couldn't see them, but he could visualize their sloven gluttony all the same. Their snouts in the mud, digging through their own waste as they hunted for anything to gobble up, inhaling it down their gullets, into their fat bellies where, ultimately, it turned into even more waste. A spreading sea of shit slowly overtaking the farm, stealing the land, turning it all into a toilet.

"Earl?" he called out again to the dark shape of a barn.

Still no answer.

Another five steps, then, plop. His foot sunk deep into the puddle and wetness seeped through his shoe, through his sock, wetting his foot. But he knew this wasn't a mud puddle. It hadn't rained in over a week. But accentuating that bit of knowledge was the odor. He'd just got shin-deep in pig shit.

"Goddammit!" he muttered, stumbling backward, shaking his foot and seeing the thick, chunky feces fling free of it. Desperate to get it off of him, off his Berluti's, his frantic movement became a sort of tribal dance.

Backstep, shake, stomp. Backstep, shake, stomp. Repeat. He even added some curse words to keep the beat.

And then, on his fifth or sixth backstep, he collided with something hard and unmoving. Had he scooted all the way to the barn? No, this mass was warm. And breathing.

The vague yeasty smell intermingled with the aroma of feces. He recognized that smell too.

"Why didn't you answer when I called out?" he asked as he made a slow circle.

The darkness made seeing impossible. Earl's face was nothing more than a black shape. Not that his expression was easy to read in the daylight.

"I brought your groceries. Those TV dinners you like. The ones with the pudding."

No response came and the man's sour demeanor further deteriorated.

"Look, if you aren't interested in speaking to me tonight, I'm going. I'll leave the food in the driveway. You can gather it yourself."

More mute, invisible observance was the only response.

The man huffed. He was tired of never being appreciated. Of everything he did being greeted with contempt rather than gratitude. "Have it your way," he said.

He began to turn back to the car when he caught a glint of silver on the ground, moonlight reflecting off metal. What's he got, the man wondered. A shovel? An ax?

Unnerved by this, his heartbeat quickened along with his pace. But he didn't make it two steps away when a hand snatched hold of the collar of his dress shirt and dragged him backward, casting him to the side like a child bored with its toy.

"Earl, you better—"

He stumbled, landing in another deep puddle of shit. However, that time he wasn't calf-deep. He hit on his side, the liquified feces sloshing across his arm, chest, shoulder. Then, no, not that—

His face.

It splashed into his eye, shot up one nostril. Only the grace of God Almighty allowed him to close his mouth just in time, but the semi-coagulated excrement smeared over his lips like chunky peanut butter.

Coughing, gagging, he stared up at Earl who loomed over him. The metal part of the tool he carried caught the moon again, another flash of silver.

"What in the hell do you thi—"

It's a scythe. He realized that as it arced through the air, soaring his direction. There was no time to think let alone react.

The blade glided across his abdomen. Painless.

Missed me, the man thought.

Then he felt the breeze against his exposed skin. And a hot, heavy wetness. His intestines began tumbling free of his midsection, hitting the puddle and its contents with a plop, plop, plop.

That's gonna cause an infection, he thought. Then Earl was grabbing him under the arms, hoisting him easily out of the puddle and off the ground. Dragging him.

The man felt his intestines unspooling behind him, an odd tugging sensation at his insides as they came free. The world went blurry, his ears hollow like his head was underwater. Despite that, he could hear the pigs.

And they were getting closer.

As his body was pressed against the fence, the hot, moist

breaths, the sticky saliva of the hogs, bombarded his skin. Then he was rising, floating. Up above the fence. Over the fence.

And then he was dropped.

The pigs swarmed him. They went for his open abdomen first, burying their faces in his wound. Snorting. Squealing. Eating.

Why'd he have to like pigs, the man thought as he stared at the Prussian blue sky, as his world began to fade away. And why'd I pick tonight to bring the groceries?

No answers came. Only the noise of the pigs and the feeling of being eaten alive.

They made quick work of his body before the sun had a chance of thinking about rising.

CHAPTER TWO

Carolina hopped out of Elven's Jeep, leaving the door hanging ajar. Despite the pain all over her body, despite lungs that still smoldered, she rushed toward Bea's door, leaving Elven behind without a word. It was rude, she knew, but at the moment there were bigger fish.

If what her mother had said on the phone was true... If Bea wasn't being Bea and turning a molehill into a mountain... If Scarlet was really in trouble.

Bea met her at the door, her eyes wet, the sclera marred by exploded vessels. She wasn't crying at this very moment, but had been recently. Crying hard and long.

Crying is for sissies, Carolina heard her mother say in her head. So who was this woman before her now?

To reinforce the surreal, doppelgänger feeling, Bea did something else that was wholly out of character. She threw her arms around Carolina and pulled her in for a firm, and excruciating, embrace.

As much as Carolina wanted to comfort Bea, her touch was akin to being caught in a vice. And without any pills to numb the pain she felt like she was going to disintegrate if she didn't break free.

So she did, pulling away from her mother quick and hard, drawing in a sharp breath as another wave of pain brought about by the movement threatened to send her to her knees.

At first, Bea's eyes narrowed in anger—there's the old Bea—but then she seemed to grasp the bigger picture and saw Carolina's battered and bloody body. The stitches. The bruises. The swelling. The soot that still lingered around her eyes, nose, and mouth like she's just spent a twelve-hour shift digging coal.

"Oh my God. What happened to you?" Bea asked.

When Carolina had seen her mother last, she'd been fresh off a few blows to the head. But now, she imagined she looked like a chew toy, reluctantly surrendered by a dog to its owner after a full day of rough play. And she felt worse than she looked.

"Don't worry about me. I'll be fine," Carolina said, wrapping her arm around her broken ribs. "Tell me what's going on."

Bea slid to the side of the doorway and motioned for her to come in. Carolina did, moving to the kitchen where she put to use one of the chairs. Bea sat across from her, hands scrabbling for a cup of coffee but shaking so hard she couldn't get a firm grip.

"Something's happened to Scarlet."

The floor creaked and Carolina glanced up to see Elven lean against the wall. He gave her a nod, reassuring her that he was there.

"Did someone call you or how—"

"No, that's just it. Your sister always calls *me*. Every Sunday and Wednesday at five. I could set my watch by her. When she didn't call Wednesday, I tried to explain it away. But I've lost track of how many times I've tried to call her since then. Texted her too. No response whatsoever. And then today." Her eyes drifted to a calendar on the wall. Birds, of course. Carolina knew she was looking at the day of the week.

"Sunday."

Then Carolina checked the stove for the time of day. 5:54.

"Did you try calling her again today?"

Bea nodded, her small head bobbing furiously. "Four times."

"Did you leave her a voicemail?"

"Of course," Bea said, her voice sharp. "I'm not a fool." Even in her distraught panic she didn't like being condescended to.

Carolina tilted her palms up in submission. "I didn't mean anything. I'm just trying to get a handle on what's happening."

"Your sister is missing! That's what's happening."

Yeah, we covered that part, Carolina thought.

"Beatrice," Elven said, stepping in and diffusing the building tension. "Have you contacted the police?"

"I wouldn't even know who to call," Bea said.

"She lives in Boston," Carolina said to Elven.

Bea huffed. "Not for three and a half years she hasn't."

That was news to Carolina who tried to think back in her head and remember the last time she'd actually exchanged more than a two line text with her half-sister. It had been a good, long while.

She supposed she should feel guilty about that, but Scarlet hadn't even sent her a card while she was in the hospital after being shot. Carolina didn't make a point of holding grudges, but the road went both ways.

"She lives in Pittsburgh now," Bea said, answering the question both Carolina and Elven had been poised to ask.

"Did she say anything the last time you two spoke that might give a reason why she wouldn't call? Problems at work? An upcoming trip?" Carolina asked.

"Nothing."

"And everything was good between you both? No arguments or..."

Bea's eyes narrowed. "No. And even if we had, she always calls me. Always." The last *always* was a more pointed, a hard jab with the sharp object of choice being her tongue.

Carolina knew what Bea meant by that. She meant Carolina never called. But apparently, Scarlet *always* called. Bea didn't have to spell it out. Carolina knew the score.

Scarlet was the favorite child.

And now it was up to the less than favorable daughter to find out what had happened to the chosen one.

"You want me to find her," she said to her mother, unsure whether it was a question or declaration. Maybe it was both.

Bea nodded.

CHAPTER THREE

"Just hold up for a minute," Elven said, trying to keep pace with Carolina as she stomped toward her van.

She didn't have the energy for a debate. Not after what she'd been through the past few weeks. Not after what she'd endured at the Weiss mansion. She threw a glance backward and found Bea standing in the doorway, wringing her hands so hard Carolina was shocked she didn't squeeze out blood.

"Get in my van," Carolina said as she crossed in front of the vehicle and dropped into the driver's seat.

Elven joined her. "What do you expect to accomplish?"

She rested her hands atop the steering wheel, taking shallow breaths that made her chest and broken ribs ache with each inhalation. "I don't know," she finally said.

"Exactly," Elven said. "Driving up there half-cocked without a plan isn't going to solve anything. You need to think this through. And I'll be glad to help."

It was a generous offer. One she knew she should accept. But when she checked the house, Bea was still there. Watching. Staring. Pleading with those distraught, foreign eyes.

"I have to go." She peeled her attention away from her mother and looked to the man at her side. The man who'd been there for her when everyone else had turned their backs. "It's my sister, Elven."

"The sister you never talk about? The sister whose very name ruins your mood? That sister?" Elven asked.

Carolina nodded. "That's the one."

"You almost died today, Carolina. You need to take time and recover. Let me make some phone calls. See what I can find out."

"I have to go," she said. But even she wasn't sure why this mattered so much. Was she trying to prove her worth to her mother? Was this an attempt to forget about the hell she'd gone through during her investigation into Cece Casto's death? Was this redemption for what happened with Lester? Or a combination of all of those, and more.

"This is foolish," Elven said, but there was resignation in his voice. He'd accepted that he'd lost. As if he ever had a chance.

"I know that. Shit, I'll probably drive all the way up there and find out that Scarlet's just pissed at Bea and ignoring her calls. Or she hooked up with some rando and went to the Poconos."

"Is that consistent with her character?"

She smiled at his cop-speak. He really was a good sheriff and she felt guilty for ever doubting him. "How the hell would I know? I haven't talked to her in years." She toyed with the keys, eager to get going. "If I find out this is all nonsense, then I can call Bea and put her mind at ease. Maybe get her to like me again."

"And if it's not? Nonsense, I mean."

"Then I guess I'll track her down." She paused, considering the gravest of possibilities. "Or find out what happened to her."

Elven paused with his hand on the door latch. "Let me ask

you. Do you think she's really missing? Or do you think Beatrice is overreacting?"

Carolina stared at the road ahead. "I have no clue. I don't know my sister. But Bea does. And I've never seen her like this."

It was Elven's turn to watch Bea who still lingered in the doorway, her gaze impatient.

"I could use some help though," Carolina said.

When Elven turned back to her, his expression was grim. "Carolina, I'd do just about anything for you. But I've got a county to care for. I can't go on some unplanned jaunt to Pennsylvania with you."

"Nothing that dramatic, Elven," she said. "I was going to ask you to extend your dog sitting services while I check into this."

He couldn't fend off a bashful smirk. "Heck. If you reclaimed Yeti, I'd be downright distraught. We've become quite the pair."

That made her feel good, to know that her shirked responsibility had somehow worked itself out for the better. The dog deserved a home, one not on wheels. And an owner who had his shit together. She could provide neither right now. Maybe—probably—never.

"Thank you."

Elven gave a quick nod. "I can do you one better too."

"How so?"

"Terrell Werner," Elven said. "He's a suit and tie type with the Pittsburgh City Police."

"Friend of yours?" she asked.

"We played ball together at WVU. Defensive lineman, built like a house."

"Great, think you can bring up your old glory days and get me some intel?"

Elven smiled, laying the charm on thick. "You're asking me,

Elven Hallie, if I can schmooze you up to someone? Of course I can do that." He unleashed a brief chortle. "I'll call him as soon as you're on the road. It'll be easier to do while you're still afar rather than in his presence."

"What the hell is that supposed to mean?" she asked.

Elven opened his door, the cool, fall air wafting inside as he dropped a foot out. "You are excellent at what you do, but you can be a little... direct. And besides that, take a second and check your reflection in the mirror."

She did. It was a rough sight.

"You look like you just came out on the losing end of a steel cage match. If you walk into the police station like that, unannounced, you're gonna be the one answering questions, not asking them."

Carolina continued to observe her image. She was no miracle worker when it came to makeup but knew she'd have to make an effort before she went out in public.

"Let me worry about that. You just make the phone call," she said.

"Alright, then." Elven finished his exit from her van, glanced at his awaiting Jeep, then back to her. "I want two promises before I let you go."

Her left leg shook, her anxiety rising along with her desire to get on the road. "What?"

"One, you remember this man is a friend of mine so please don't be too much of a thorn in his butt."

"I'll try."

"Suppose that's about as good as I can expect," Elven said. "What's the second?"

"That you'll be careful."

She didn't want to lie to him, so she didn't promise that.

CHAPTER FOUR

She drove four hours before the exhaustion from the day's events hit like a Mack truck. Rather than fall asleep at the wheel and crash, she pulled into a rest stop, meaning to steal a cat nap. Instead she woke up with the sun battering her eyes. A check of the time showed it was almost eight a.m. She'd slept for almost twelve straight hours.

It was her first good night's sleep in longer than she could remember, but it was time to get back on the highway. Ninety minutes later, she was there.

The air in Pittsburgh was cool and damp as wind glided over the rivers. It cut through her as she strode across the parking lot. Ahead stood a dirty, yellow brick building upon which Pittsburgh Bureau of Police was emblazoned in block letters. It was old and industrial, weathered and tired, and fit in perfectly with the city, or at least as much as she'd observed on the drive in.

As she was buzzed inside, she was struck with an odd sense of deja vu even though she'd never been there in her life. It was because it reminded Carolina of her station in Baltimore.

A steady drone of forms being filed, telephones being answered, uniformed officers coming and going. The memories summoned by returning to this type of scene weren't exactly fond, but there was a comfortable familiarity.

The feeling dissipated when she began to catch curious, too long stares as she pushed deeper into the building. As the workers observed her not as one of their own, but as an outsider and all the potential danger that came with the unknown. Carolina tucked her head, trying to hide her damaged face, as she slid into line at the front desk.

The woman ahead of her reeked of menthol cigarettes and toe fungus, the latter even more pungent because she wore flip flops even though the temperature outdoors hadn't gone beyond sixty. Carolina stared at the woman's misshapen, dirty feet. The nail on one of her big toes looked like a piece of cork hot glued in place in a sort of macabre crafting accident.

"Have a seat and you'll be called shortly, ma'am," the officer behind the window said to the woman. He was middle-aged and wore his hair buzzed close to hide that he was losing it.

"What?" the woman asked, planting her forearms on a ledge meant for signing papers, not holding body weight. It gave a low, plaintive moan. "How long will it take? I got things to do."

Like see a podiatrist, Carolina thought.

The officer put on one of the fakest smiles Carolina had ever seen. "Shouldn't be more than ten, fifteen minutes, Ms. Pyle."

The woman huffed. "This is bullshit." She spun around, pushing past Carolina and plopping into a gold-colored chair, already on her cell phone even though less than six seconds had passed. "You ain't gonna believe this shit—"

"Next," the officer said.

Carolina told him who she was and that she was there to

see Terrell Werner and after a long, suspicious look to ensure his leg wasn't being pulled, the officer grabbed his phone.

"Sergeant Werner. I have a Carolina McKay here. Says you're expecting her." His dull, brown eyes met Carolina's and the doubt left them. He even managed a real smile. "Alright. I'll send her up."

As she moved to follow the officer's directions, Carolina heard the woman in the flip flops throw shade. "Ain't that about right. Skinny white bitch gets sent straight in while the rest of us get told to wait our place."

Carolina tried not to cringe, or laugh, and surprised herself by succeeding at both.

TERRELL WERNER TOWERED over Carolina even while sitting in his orthopedic office chair. His plus-sized body blocked all light from entering the room via the window behind him, leaving the overhead fluorescents to do the job.

And he laughed, a sound like a sonic boom in the cramped office with its low acoustic ceilings and paneled walls.

"So Elven stood there, naked as the day he was born, covering his crotch with both hands while that old cop stared us down," he said, catching his breath.

She sat there, struggling to remain patient but simultaneously relieved that the man was willing to talk to her, to help her, in this city where she knew no one.

Werner continued, "And then Elven said, 'No officer. It's not a groundhog. It's a pineapple.'"

The giant of a man went into another laughing fit. His bulky biceps pushed the sleeves of his off-the-rack dress shirt to their limits. The way the material stretched across his back, it was easy to imagine the cloth tearing away like a Black version of the Incredible Hulk if he ever became angry.

She smiled, mildly amused. The story wasn't half-bad and she'd be sure to use it to take Elven down a peg the next time she needed ammunition, but she hadn't come to Pittsburgh to listen to old college football stories.

"That's great," she said, hoping to be past the pleasantries and superficial bonding. "But I'd really appreciate it if you could help me out with filing the missing person's report on my sister."

Werner sat straighter in his chair, using his pinky finger to wipe away a gleeful tear that had escaped his eye. "Of course," he said. "About that."

He turned to his computer, tapping at the keyboard. Within seconds any semblance of a smile was gone and Carolina felt her stomach tighten into a ball. She wasn't sure she could handle more bad news.

"Seems we missed the boat," Werner said.

"What do you mean?" she asked, wary of the answer. But if Scarlet had been found dead in a dumpster or floating in the Monongahela, surely he wouldn't have started this meeting off with jokes. Right?

"I mean there's already a report on Scarlet Tanager Engle. It was filed six days ago."

Carolina realized she'd been holding her breath and let it out, fluttering some of the papers on the big man's desk. "Oh."

"Sorry if I scared you," he said.

"You didn't," she lied. "Who reported her missing?"

"Well," he said, then paused too long as he chose his words carefully. "That's the rub. It's not a missing person's report. Not in the traditional sense."

She leaned into the desk, trying to steal a glance at his computer screen but it was too far off axis. "Then what sense is it?"

Werner's lips pressed together as he chewed them before answering. "It's an all-points bulletin."

"What the fuck are you talking about?" She was on her feet, turning the computer screen toward her. She saw her sister's name, then Federal Bureau—

Before she could read more, Werner's hand was atop hers. It was oppressive in its bulk and strength and he easily moved the screen out of her line of sight. "I'd appreciate it if you return to your seat. And that you don't do that again."

She wanted to jump out of her skin, but obeyed, remembering Elven's plea to be nice to his old pal.

"Sorry," she managed. "You just can't imagine how stressful this is."

Werner seemed to consider that and softened. "You're right about that. I can't imagine."

"So, what can you tell me?"

He shifted his gaze to the screen, lips moving in silence as he read. It was a long wait until he spoke. "This appears to have originated at her place of employment."

"Where's that?" Carolina asked.

His right eye narrowed, but then he nodded. "I get it. My family's a once a year at Christmas kind of deal too."

"Ours is a little less frequent," she said, trying to remember the last time she and Scarlet had spoken in person. It was at a funeral, but she couldn't even recall whose.

"Yet you drove all the way up here nevertheless?" he asked, studying her.

"We're still family. She and our mother are close, but I'm more on the outskirts. So, no, we don't make a habit of chatting about our daily activities, but that doesn't mean I don't care about her."

There it was. All laid out. It was about as honest as she could be with a stranger. Although, in some ways, it was easier to be honest with a stranger than it was to those who knew her.

Werner nodded and looked at the monitor. "She was employed by Golden Waters Casino."

"Was she a witness to something? Is that why they're looking for her?"

Werner gave his plus-sized head a slow shake. "I'm not at liberty to say."

"Come on, Sergeant. I'm not just family. I was a detective in Baltimore. I know how the system works."

"I'm aware," Werner said. "Elven told me all about you."

"He did?"

Werner nodded. "He also told me to brace myself because, in his words, you're a hurricane in a jar."

All things considered, she took that as a compliment. "So you know my story. All I'm asking for is some professional courtesy."

He leaned back in his chair. "I would if I could. Truly. But this is all well above my pay grade."

She tried to read between the lines and thought she had a bead on what might be happening. "Is Scarlet involved in a crime?"

Werner sighed. "Let me end our conversation with this. From what I've read, my belief is that Ms. Engle is missing by choice."

"And that's all you'll say?" she asked.

"It is. I'm sorry."

Carolina stood. "You should be."

So much for playing nice.

CHAPTER FIVE

Carolina parked the van a block down from the Riverview Heights apartment complex. Before she'd left Dupray, Bea had given her the spare key to Scarlet's apartment along with the address, but now that she'd arrived she double-checked to ensure she was at the right place. She wasn't aware she'd come here with expectations, but she had and they were exceeded.

The place was towering, shiny, and new. It wouldn't have stood out in New York or Miami, but in Pittsburgh, it was very high end. As she strolled by a gated parking lot accessible only by key card, she saw rows of Mercedes, BMWs, and Audis. She threw a glance back at her van, her home. She wondered, with some jealousy, how the hell her little sister, who had passed high school with a C minus average, had climbed so high.

As she continued to the entrance, she contemplated the story she was going to tell the doorman, who stood by double glass doors, reading a paperback novel. He was in his seventies, clad in a suit and a dapper, pink bow tie. In the end, she made the rare decision to go with the truth.

With her best smile on her bruised face, she cleared her throat to get the man's attention. It didn't work so she took another step and went for it again.

That time he heard her, peering at her from behind overgrown eyebrows that shaded his baby blues. She was relieved when he returned her smile.

"Good morning, miss," the doorman said, his voice bordering on fragile.

"Good morning to you too. My sister lives here and I thought I'd stop by and surprise her."

His grin widened revealing dentures. "How nice of you. And your sister's name?"

"Scarlet," Carolina said. Then added, "Scarlet Tanager Engle."

"Oh yes," he said. "Miss Engle is always so sweet. I can't say that for all our tenants." He gave an exaggerated chuckle and Carolina laughed politely.

"I can only imagine," she said.

He punched a code into the keypad beside the door, then began to open it for her. She felt guilty about this elderly man waiting on her and reached for him but he waved her off.

"Now, now," he said. "I'm not too feeble to hold the door for a beautiful woman. The day I am is the day I retire."

That brought about a real laugh. Then she remembered he probably expected a tip and she dug for her money clip, extracted a five, and passed it to him. She thought he seemed disappointed and she wondered what the going rate was for doormen at swanky apartment buildings. Apparently beyond her budget.

As she passed through the door he called out. "It's been some time since I've seen Miss Engle. We must be working opposite shifts. Please tell her Walter sends his regards."

"I will," Carolina said, moving onto the lobby which was full of marble or granite, she never could tell the difference, with towering ceilings and white leather furniture scattered about. Enormous oil paintings, mostly cityscapes, decorated the walls. A woman in a designer power suit strode past her, taking a long and judgmental look. Carolina considered flipping her the bird, maybe even doubling up, but held back and tried to blend in.

The elevator played classical music as she rode to the sixth floor and she rechecked her appearance in the mirrored ceiling. Considering what she'd been through the last few days, she wasn't that bad.

When the swelling went down in a day or two, she'd be right as rain. The stab wound in her arm, the broken ribs... those would take a little longer.

God, how she wished Elven hadn't flushed all her pills. Two or three of those would be worth triple their weight in gold right about now.

As she calculated the odds of convincing one of her doctors to phone in a prescription to a Pittsburgh pharmacy, the elevator reached its destination and the doors glided open. Everything worked smooth as butter, not like the herky jerky movements of the lift in her old apartment building in Baltimore. That one was like riding a hundred-year-old roller coaster and she'd said a prayer of thanks every time she didn't plummet to her death. Back when she cared about such things.

Scarlet's apartment, suite 665, was at the far end of the hall —a corner unit. Those were always the most expensive as you had the luxury of windows on two walls, and again, all she could think was *What the fuck?*

She didn't bother with a knock, unlocking the door and letting herself inside. If the lobby and building were a ten, then Scarlet's condo was a ten thousand. It looked like something out of a magazine with luxury furniture that was built purely for aesthetics, scorning comfort. It felt almost futuristic in its exotic, minimalist style. Everything looked sterile and soulless, yet ridiculously expensive.

"Who the hell lives like this?" she whispered. "Who are you, Scarlet?"

She let the door close behind her, though not fully latching, as she moved deeper into the condo. The floor-to-ceiling windows provided a panoramic view of the city. From there Carolina could see the sports stadiums, bridges, more bridges. Cities had never been her thing, even when living in them, but she knew this was a very expensive view.

The apartment, as she'd expected, was void of people. A quick check of the fridge showed fruit that had gone soft and a molding loaf of French bread sat atop the island. Her sister hadn't been here in a week, maybe longer.

Carolina needed to understand who her sister was and the best way to unravel a woman was to explore her bedroom, so that's where she headed. The bed was covered in pillows, duvets, comforters. She knew all these things served purposes, but they were lost on a girl who lived in a van and slept on a secondhand Serta.

Nonetheless she couldn't resist dragging her fingers across fabric so white it was almost virginal. It felt smooth as glass, soft as a cloud. It was painfully hard to resist the urge to flop onto it, to rut around like a pig in slop and enjoy the excesses, but she did. For now.

The nightstand was bereft of photos, notepads, of anything personal. Carolina could tell there were two drawers in it but no handles with which to open them. It was like some sort of puzzle box and the dull ache in her head kicked itself into a higher gear as she ran her fingers along the seams and tried to solve the mystery. Then, as a last resort, she pushed against the top drawer.

Inside came a click and then the drawer eased itself open with the kind of drama only known to stupidly expensive furniture. But it was a bust. The only contents were a few pens, a handful of condoms, hand sanitizer, and some mints.

Carolina sat on the edge of the bed and gave the drawer a light push. Once it closed she moved on to the bottom compartment. Its only contents were a wooden, black box. A jewelry box, Carolina assumed. Wondering what diamonds and gold she might find inside, she opened the lid when—

"What are you doing in here?" a man's voice echoed through the sprawling room.

Surprised, Carolina dropped the box which clattered to the carpeted floor, the lid springing open, and the contents—a vibrating dildo that came to life in the fall—spilling free.

She looked to the man who'd barked at her, found him staring, studying. Then his eyes went to the floor—to the dildo. It wriggled like a wounded snake, clattering against Carolina's shoe, then moved in the opposite direction.

The man's face flared red and Carolina imagined hers matched his shade. She quickly kicked the dildo under the bed, hard. It bounced off the wall on the other side and mercifully stopped vibrating.

Then they stared at each other. The black suit he wore was polyester and ill-fitting. Not that she was judging, she just knew cheap clothes when she saw them because she was a bargain rack shopper. But his clothes alerted her to an important fact.

He too did not live in this building.

"Are you going to answer my question?" he asked, arms crossed over his chest.

"What was that again?"

"What are you doing in this apartment?"

"I should ask you the same thing. What are you, maintenance?" She knew he wasn't but thought a well-timed dig would help her keep the upper hand.

He uncrossed his arms, took a step toward her. "Look, I think we got off on the wrong foot here."

"Yeah," Carolina said. "That tends to happen when someone enters my sister's apartment without so much as a knock at the door."

His tired eyes widened. "You're Scarlet Engle's sister?"

She didn't like the tone of his voice. It wasn't only skeptical, it bordered on bewilderment. She also didn't like how he looked her up and down. "I am," she said.

"I never would've guessed. She's a lot—"

"Think very carefully about your phrasing," Carolina said.

"Blonder," the man settled on.

"Fair enough," she said.

"Now it's your turn. Who are you?"

Instead of answering, he reached into his jacket and on instinct, her hand flew to her gun, drawing and aiming before he could so much as blink. She held the pistol, trained on his chest, but he seemed nonplussed. A wry, humorless smile pulled at the right side of his mouth, twisting his small mustache askew.

"Don't shoot me," he said. "It won't look good on your file."

"What the fuck are you talking about?" she asked, easing her finger away from the trigger but keeping it close, in case.

"You're a cop, right?"

"I used to be," she said.

"I could tell. You have that whole, shoot first, ask questions later approach to dealing with a situation. I'm FBI and unlike your kind, we have rules to follow."

He went into his jacket pocket and his hand emerged with a badge. Even at a distance Carolina knew it was the real deal and she holstered her gun.

"Special Agent Jack Burrell," he said, re-pocketing his badge. "And that makes you Carolina McKay." It was a statement, not a question. He'd done his research. But he stared at her face, her injuries.

"I've had a rough couple of days," she said.

"I see that."

As she rose from the bed, it was her turn to examine him. Jack Burrell was maybe a decade or so older than her, somewhere in his mid to late forties, but seemed older due to the bags under his eyes and the deep wrinkles that crisscrossed his forehead. A smattering of stubble decorated his cheeks and his hair had that *just rolled out of bed and too lazy to use a comb* kind of look. He stood a shade over six feet in height and had the build of a scarecrow.

He dug into his pants pocket and pulled out a Dum Dum Lollipop—watermelon flavored—removed the wrapper, and popped it in his mouth. "Want one?"

Carolina shook her head. This was the best the Feds had to offer?

"Quit smoking last winter," Jack said as if reading her mind.

"Good for you. Now why don't you try telling me why the FBI is so interested in my little sister."

He grinned, revealing gums that were already stained pink from the lolli. "I can give you three hundred thousand reasons."

CHAPTER SIX

Another day, another diner. It seemed, for Carolina, every meeting of importance happened over food and this one was no different.

She sat across from Jack Burrell who studied the menu with the concentration of a man reading a *how to defuse bombs* manual. The duo was crammed into a back booth at Wojcik's Eatery which had a bustling lunch crowd comprised of loud, squawking patrons who made it hard to think.

She hadn't so much as glanced at her own laminated menu. The sign as they've entered promised Award-Winning Pierogies and that was good enough for her.

The waiter, a teen with an acne laden face and bifocals, sidled up next to their station with pad and pen in hand. He spoke not a word and Carolina wasn't sure if this was the worst customer service she'd ever received, or if it was the best thing ever.

Just take the order and avoid the chitchat, his eyes said.

The silence had a type of magic to it and she made a mental note to add a buck to his tip.

Jack went first. "Give me two of the triple bacon burgers. Do those come with barbecue sauce?" Jack looked up at the kid as he wrote the order down. He was met with only a nod. "Double order of fries with beef gravy. An order of chicken fingers with ranch. Two blueberry muffins. A side of applesauce with plenty of cinnamon." He kept staring at the menu. "And a chocolate egg cream."

The kid turned to Carolina, expectant.

"Onion and cheddar pierogies," she said. "Slathered in butter. And a large Diet Coke, no ice."

The kid nodded and disappeared.

"Quite the waiter we have there," Jack said, looking Carolina over. "I didn't know the Irish ate pierogies."

"I didn't know I was Irish," she said.

"I just assumed. The last name, your pale skin. The hair. Kind of stereotypical Black Irish, don't you think?"

She stared at him waiting to find a point. Instead he took a swig of coffee.

"That food you ordered," she said. "You have an invisible partner or something?"

"Intermittent fasting," he said, like that was supposed to mean something to her. When he saw it didn't, he continued. "I only eat one meal a day. Keeps your metabolism guessing. I've lost eighty-five pounds in the last year."

"Shit," she said, trying not to let her eyes grow wide and reveal that she was impressed.

"Besides, Uncle Sam's buying. He's picking up your tab too. Hell of a guy, he is."

She thought about protesting, decided against it. "Alright, so when are you gonna tell me what you were doing at my sister's? And what's going on with her?"

He switched gears from grinning to game face. Very professional, she had to give him that. "The Golden Waters

Casino contacted the FBI a couple months back when they realized just shy of thirty grand had gone missing."

"Seems like small potatoes for a casino. Thirty thousand could be an accounting error."

Jack swirled the coffee in his cup. "Yeah, that's what we thought too. Then another thirty went missing three weeks after. And thirty more the beginning of October. That's when I got sent to the City of Rivers."

"Sounds exciting," she said, hoping her sarcasm came through.

If it did, he missed it. "Not really. It's all legwork. Reviewing their financials. Then interviewing everyone who works at the place. Not exactly the kind of stuff they sell you on when they recruit you for the agency."

He'd emphasized those last few words and she knew he was trying to impress her. It didn't work.

"Okay?"

"When I say everyone, I mean everyone. From the illegals who scrub the bathroom floors to the guy in the sharkskin suit who runs the place. I was about three days in when I got to your sister."

"What is she? A cocktail waitress?"

It was Jack's turn to give her a questioning stare. "You don't know what your own sister does for a living?"

Carolina sighed. "Why's that such a big deal? We aren't close. Our mother hasn't heard from her and sent me to check. What else do you want to know, Dr. Phil?"

Jack cleared his throat. "Thank God the agency never assigned me a female partner."

Carolina sighed, a mix of laughter and disbelief. It was tempting to rip into him, but between the anxiety and pain she couldn't work up the anger to bother.

"Anyway," Jack started. "I questioned Miss Engle—your sister that works at the casino," he emphasized with a smirk. "She didn't raise any alarm bells, but the next day she didn't show up for work. Nor the day after that. Or the next. And no one's seen her since."

"That's all you've got?" Carolina asked. "She ditched a crap job and that means she absconded with a hundred K?"

Jack poured another cream into his mug. "I see where you're coming from. But the day I interviewed her, more money went missing. Not thirty thousand this time either. Two hundred thousand."

Carolina stared, not saying anything. And not admitting that the luxurious apartment and its furnishings seemed to make more sense when adding this news to the equation.

"How's that for a smoking gun?" he asked.

The waiter appeared at their table before she could respond. With lanky arms he distributed the food then left them, wordless.

Jack chomped a huge bite out of burger number one. Barbecue sauce oozed from it, trickling down his chin, clinging to the stubble there. He wiped it away with his fingers then sucked them clean.

"Classy," she said.

"What's that waiter's deal anyway?" he asked after swallowing the massive bite of beef and bun. "You think he doesn't like me?"

"I'm sure he wouldn't be the first," she said.

Jack ignored her. "So, what's your read on the missing money situation? Does any of this sound like your sister?"

She halved a pierogi with her fork and pushed it into her mouth to avoid answering straight off. She wanted to say no, that there was absolutely no way that Scarlet would steal three hundred thousand dollars. Or any amount of dollars. But the reality was, she had no idea who Scarlet was.

"Half-sister," she said, though she wasn't sure why that was important now. She'd been referring to Scarlet as her sister all afternoon.

But she knew the reason.

She was trying to make herself feel better for not knowing anything about her. Trying to distance herself from the woman suspected of being a thief.

"And as to whether this is something my sister could do..." She poked at her food, trying to rejuvenate her appetite. "I have no clue."

CHAPTER SEVEN

Carolina had never been to Las Vegas or Atlantic City. Never been inside any casino. But she'd seen them in films and on TV and was always a little in awe at the glittery excesses, the spectacle, the untethered, freewheeling fun.

She expected the same vibe as she approached the Golden Waters Casino. The outside fit, plenty of glass reflecting the lights and the river rushing by. She actually felt her pulse quicken as she approached the doors, passing a Hummer limo along the way.

But stepping inside was like entering another dimension, one where joy had been outlawed. Senior citizens on motorized scooters cruised along at two miles per hour. College students, so drunk they couldn't sit up straight, crowded blackjack tables and roulette wheels. The middle-aged crowd favored the slot machines, pumping in quarter after quarter with dazed, half-closed eyes.

A dense cloud of cigarette smoke filled the joint and moving through it was like walking into a blue fog, one that tightened her lungs and burned her eyes. Carolina was hurting already and felt as if a few hours in this place would send her to her grave.

A waitress skirted the floor, prancing around in a black dress that hugged her curves. She seemed more alive than most in the place, with rouge-rosy cheeks that held a perpetual smile. Carolina wondered how it was possible to maintain cheer in a place so grim, then realized that grumps don't get tipped.

"Excuse me," Carolina said with a quick wave to catch the girl's attention.

She was in her mid-twenties with permed red hair and curls that bounced as she approached. Her hair wasn't all that bounced either and Carolina's eyes fell to her ample bosom, which was probably the point.

"Did you need a drink, hon?" she asked. Her voice was so high pitched and chipper that she could have done cartoon voice-over work on the side.

"No, I'm actually looking for the manager," Carolina said.

"Oh. Which one do you need? Bar, floor, guest services..."

"Someone who oversees exchanging cash for chips and vice versa? Customer relations, maybe?"

Earlier Jack had told her that Scarlet worked in *the cage*. At first she'd taken that to mean she was some kind of stripper, suspended above the gambling floor and shedding her clothes for the plebeians below. He had to explain that the job consisted of paying out winnings, among other tasks.

"You want Randy then," she said, glancing toward the back right corner. "If you head past the poker tables, there's the cage over there." She flashed a smile so perfect it could have been in a Colgate commercial. "Want me to lead the way?"

"I can manage," Carolina said.

The waitress waited, staring at Carolina, expectant with her empty tray in hand, and Carolina caught on. She was waiting for gratitude in the form of cash.

"Thanks for the help," Carolina said, spinning around and leaving the girl in her wake.

Soon enough she found a bleach-blonde woman perched behind a large set of bars with a slot underneath, and a large divot in the counter.

"The cage," Carolina said, finally understanding the name.

The woman stacked large piles of cash into perfect pillars. "Beg pardon," she said.

"Nothing," Carolina said. "A waitress sent me over here, told me to—"

Blondie groaned and muttered, "Goddamn." She looked up from the cash with bloodshot eyes and a sour expression. "Lost my count cause of you."

"Sorry," Carolina said, even though she wasn't. "I'm looking for Randy."

Blondie took a long, skeptical look, then shrugged. "If you say so." She half-turned on her stool and barked, "Randy!" in a hoarse tenor.

As if on command, a door behind Blondie sprung open and a man with a patchy beard poked his head through the opening.

"What's going on?" His voice was reedy and nervous and Carolina wondered how this schlub of a man could be in charge of anything, let alone large sums of cash.

"Lady here wants you," the Blondie said, then resumed her counting.

The door opened further and Randy Drake shuffled through. He dragged the back of his hand across a greasy forehead, then wiped that hand clean on his shirt. His mouse-brown hair was pulled back into a tight ponytail and Carolina could see spots of eczema attacking the follicles. When his eyes found Carolina, he smiled, showing off vaguely yellow choppers.

"Hello," he said. "How can I be of service?"

Carolina peered at him through the bars. He looked to be

around forty, but his complexion was still that of a teen. "I need to talk to you about an issue with an employee."

Blondie glanced up, wary.

"Not you," Carolina said.

Blondie looked back to the cash and Carolina heard her groan as she started over again.

"In private, if possible," Carolina said to Randy.

He nodded and opened the side door, stepping out and latching it behind him. He waved her to follow and he plopped down at an empty blackjack table. Carolina sat across from him, close enough so she could hear him, but not so close to feel his eyes crawling all over her.

Before they got started, Randy lifted a hand and summoned a waitress. This one was dressed in the same tight-fitting dress, but had a few more miles on her.

"Bring me over a seltzer," Randy said. "You?" he asked Carolina. "It's on the house."

"Diet Coke."

The waitress nodded and walked off. Randy's eyes drifted to her rear end as she moved away and he chewed his bottom lip like it was a piece of taffy. He didn't stop ogling until Carolina cleared her throat.

His eyes snapped to her. "What can I help you with, miss?" Randy asked. "I hope none of my staff treated you poorly. If they did, I assure you—"

"Nothing like that," Carolina said. "I'm here to talk about Scarlet Engle."

Randy's lascivious gaze cooled. "Oh. Are you with the FBI, too?"

"I'm not an agent, but I am working with them," she said. A little lie never hurt anyone.

"Alright, then what do you need? I told that guy, Burrell, everything. Not that there was much to tell."

Carolina nodded. "I understand. I know the facts, but I'm

trying to dig a little deeper. To get a feel for Scarlet. Figure out what makes her tick. It might help us locate her."

"If you say so," he said. "We weren't like, pals, so I don't know that I can be a lot of help, but you ask what you want to ask and I'll give you the God's honest in return."

"Let's start with her personality. Did you like her?"

His eyes narrowed, suspicious. "How do you mean that?"

"I'm not inferring anything untoward, I promise. Was she easy to work with? Did she play well with others? That kind of thing."

Randy took a deep breath and pulled his sweat-soaked shirt away from his man boobs, but it snapped back in place, hugging his curves. Carolina studied him, trying to decide whether he was nervous or simply a big man in a too-small shirt stuck in a hot room.

"I mean, she was alright," he said with a shrug. "Did her job. Never caused any problems. My only issue with her was a lack of motivation."

"How so?"

"Well, most of the workers, you offer them overtime and they say, *Yes, sir, as much as I can get.* But she'd never come in early or stay late. Wouldn't work the weekends either even though that pays an extra three bucks an hour."

"Was she full time?"

"Nah. Twenty-five hours a week and not a minute more."

"Did she have any other jobs at the casino? Before working in your department?"

He shook his head. "Nope. I was surprised she didn't waitress. Pays a hell of a lot better than the cage."

"Really?" She was surprised a service job would be higher paying than one that required handling vast sums of cash.

"Yeah," Randy said. "Cause of the tips. Hourly rate's about the same, but a good-lookin—" He swallowed the word down. "A good waitress can clear an extra hundred, hundred fifty a night in tips. You don't get that in the cage. I told her all that, but she blew me off like I was selling snozzberries."

Carolina looked to Blondie who was still counting bills. She wore a boxy vest, with a short sleeve shirt underneath. It was the opposite of provocative.

"Maybe she wasn't a fan of the servers' uniforms," Carolina offered.

Randy fought back a leer but only half-succeeded. "Yeah, the waitresses wear minis, but what's the big deal? They got on more clothes than the girls at Hooters."

About that time the older waitress returned with their drinks and Carolina took a second glance at the attire. The dress wasn't only skin tight, it was so short that bending over would have raised the rating from PG-13 to R.

"Anything else?" she asked, her voice filled with tired disinterest.

It was a no from both and she headed for greener pastures.

Carolina downed half her soda in a long swallow. "How was her attendance? Was she reliable? On time?"

Randy burped, loud and long. "That's the one thing I have to give her credit on. She never missed a shift. Never called out sick or no-showed. But like I said, this gig was strictly a daytime thing for her. I figured maybe she moonlighted somewhere."

"Any ideas where?"

He shook his head, eyes drifting away from her, losing interest. "I don't make a habit of asking my girls about their personal lives."

My girls. In your dreams maybe.

Carolina found it hard to believe that this slimeball respected personal boundaries, but also doubted there was anything else to be gained from the man so it was time to put them both out of their shared misery.

"Is there anyone here who might be able to tell me more about her?"

He finished his seltzer, climbing to his feet. "Don't know. She was a bit of a cold fish. Not very personable. I never really saw her hang out with anyone."

That wasn't the Scarlet Carolina remembered. The younger, high school version of her half-sister was outgoing, the life of the party, much to their mother's delight. Scarlet was her Mini Me. "Really? She didn't associate with anyone?"

Randy Drake shrugged his broad shoulders. "I don't know. Maybe try Suzette." He pointed his nose toward Blondie. "They worked the same shift most of the time. She has a break coming up in about half an hour if you can wait around."

It wasn't like she had anything better to do.

CHAPTER EIGHT

"Knew she was trouble from the day she started," Suzette Pizer said, the words coming out along with a cloud of cigarette smoke.

It was quite a lead, especially since Carolina hadn't got around to asking any questions yet.

"Trouble how?" Carolina asked.

"Fake for one thing. Fake as her fingernails. Tits too, probably."

Carolina stifled a laugh. She didn't know much about her sister's current life but she knew the woman had no need for breast augmentation.

Suzette took a drag on her cig. "Nothing good comes from those types. They flirt around with the bosses, always fawning all over 'em like they're King of Shit Kingdom, but it's all fake. All so they can get away with something. For most of the girls that's just being lazy. Clocking in late, leaving early. But obviously Scarlet had grander plans. And here we are." She spread her hands out as if revealing the punch line to a magic trick.

"What does that mean?" Carolina asked, but she already knew Suzette had Scarlet tried and convicted.

"It means that she took that money. It's obvious. And you know what, for someone as friendly as she was, she sure didn't want to help that many customers. She always pawned them off on me."

She leaned in to Carolina, sending gusts of her coffee laden breath her way.

"That girl, she made me do the busywork so I'd be distracted and wouldn't see her hiding the money. Makes sense, don't it?"

Carolina nodded. It wasn't that she agreed with Suzette, but when a fish was on a hook you wanted to keep them there.

"So, let's say she hid the money while you're tied up with customer service. How does she get it out of the casino without being noticed? That kind of cash... It's not like shoving a hundred dollar bill in your bra."

Suzette half-laughed, half-coughed. "That's the kicker, ain't it? Scarlet was, hmm, how should I put it delicately? A whore. Like I said, she flirted with the bosses, all the male ones anyway."

"Even Randy?" Carolina pushed.

"Especially Randy. I've seen how he looks at her. Heart-shaped ass pushed against her skirt, bending over in front of him to get money from the lock box. Doesn't take a genius to see what she was doing. And Randy, love the man and God bless him, but all his brains are in his Fruit of the Looms if you catch my drift."

"So she flirts with Randy, maybe promises him a happy ending or something, in exchange for him looking the other way while she walks out with the money?" Carolina asked.

Suzette's eyes narrowed. "That's not what I said at all, honey. Maybe all those bruises on your face caused you to get some ear damage, too." She smiled revealing a set of nicotine-stained dentures.

Carolina gritted her teeth and managed a placating grin.

"What I'm saying is she used her womanly bits to distract people. You get 'em looking at your tits or ass and they don't see what your hands are doing. Like a slutty David Copperfield." She tapped ash from her smoke. "Randy liked to look, maybe too much. That's a man for you. But not for one moment do I think he'd risk his job for her. He was just a pawn."

The story seemed implausible, but Carolina let her go on.

"You ask me, I say it went down like this. Scarlet had the money hid somewhere in the cage. Her shift ends, she clocks out and heads for the exit. Finds one of the nice guards, the ones who got good hearts but low IQs. She engages in some small-talk, smiles, laughs at their bad jokes. Probably rubs their arm. Then she goes, 'Oh, I forgot my purse. I have to go back for it. Can you leave the door unlocked, handsome?' They agree because they're men and they're stupid and," she spread her hands out again, "voilà. She sashays her ass out with a bag full of cash."

"Any particular guard you think would fall for that?" Carolina asked.

Suzette shrugged. "I ain't sayin' that any of them were in on it with her, mind you. They all got hearts of gold, but a young thing like that, stroking biceps, giggling like a schoolgirl, that shit can break a man. Believe me, I used to be able to pull that stuff off a few years back, too. Not that I did, mind you."

Carolina looked the woman over. A few years? Suzette was either delusional, or had aged hard and fast. She saw little to no truth in the woman's fantastical tale, and didn't want to waste more time on her especially when withdrawal had her feeling ready to barf. If she wanted to accomplish anything here, she needed to remedy that.

CHAPTER NINE

After fifteen minutes of scouring the casino floor, Carolina found her mark. The woman sat at the slots, submitting quarter after quarter to the one armed bandit. A fat, white neck brace gave her head a free-floating appearance and she wore a removable leg cast over her Steelers sweatpants.

Carolina approached. Time to get on with the getting on.

"Excuse me, ma'am," she said and the woman peeled her eyes off the machine.

She was in her late fifties, hair pulled in a gray topknot. Her glassy eyes told Carolina she'd picked a good target. "Yeah?"

Carolina took a deep breath. Lying was a skill she's near perfected, but even for her, what was to come was a doozy. "I'm undercover security for the casino. One of our surveillance techs," she tipped her head to one of the many cameras that pointed down from the ceiling, "has reason to believe you have a recording device in your purse."

The woman's eyes widened in alarm. "I don't know—"

"Please," Carolina said, holding up her hand. "I don't want

to turn this into a scene and bring any attention to you, but I do need to search your bag."

The woman's brows knitted together as she considered this. "If you refuse, we'll need to get the police involved."

That seemed to make up her mind. "Go ahead then," the woman said, unmoving, frozen on her stool. "But I didn't do anything. I don't know what they," her eyes went to the cameras, "think they saw but all I got in there—"

Again Carolina held up her palm. Shush.

She took the woman's bag, and made a ninety degree turn so that her own body was between the gambler and her purse.

Her hands rummaged, quick and no nonsense. She had little interest in the compact, the cigarettes, the silver flask. There was a brush so full of shedded hair that she needed to stifle a gag, a few tubes of lipstick and mascara, a tin of Altoids. She was beginning to lose hope, to think this embarrassing charade was for naught, but then she found it.

A perfect, orange prescription bottle. One look at the label and her heartbeat quickened.

Percocet.

Salvation in pill form. Hallelujah.

Carolina palmed the bottle, deftly slipping it into her jacket pocket as she turned back to the woman who was so anxious her whole body trembled.

"Well?" the gambler asked.

"It appears our tech was mistaken," Carolina said as she handed the woman her bag. "I'm very sorry for the inconvenience." She reached into another pocket, grabbed her money clip, and peeled off a hundred dollar bill which she passed to the woman. "Please accept this as a token of Golden Waters Casino's appreciation."

With a bony hand the woman snatched it, a giddy smile on her face. "Shit. You can search my bag any day if I get a Benjamin Franklin in return."

Carolina smiled, polite and professional. "Enjoy your time and good luck."

The gambler was already back at the machine, now with renewed vigor and free money to lose.

Carolina considered feeling bad for the theft, decided against it, and headed to the bathroom.

SHE CHEWED two Percs and took a drink straight from the faucet to wash the bitter taste from her mouth. In the time it took her to go from the sink to the door she was already feeling like herself again. Her head clear, she saw little sense hanging around the casino, talking to people who seemed to know nothing about her sister.

What she needed to do was return to Scarlet's apartment and complete the deep dive Jack Burrell had interrupted. There had to be something helpful. Mail, cards, a date book, anything that could lead her to people who were actually involved in her sister's life, not those who only existed on the periphery.

She'd almost made it to the main exit when she heard the voice.

"Miss?" the man called.

Carolina shot a glance over her shoulder and saw a middle-aged, bald man in a suit so shiny it looked waterproof. His eyes were locked on her and his long strides closed the distance fast.

But she kept moving, quickening her own pace.

"Miss?"

That time she didn't look back, only ahead. Twenty yards away from the exit. Fifteen.

Around ten she felt his hand on her shoulder. Damn it all.

She shook herself free as she gave up and turned to face him.

He looked her up and down, inspecting, examining. "I've been looking for you," he said. "Almost got away on me."

Fuck. She'd pressed her luck going with that security ruse. Now she was the one who got busted by the eye in the sky. How was she going to talk her way out of this mess?

"I'm sorry, I'm in a bit of a rush," she said. "Had a call from work, they need me to come in early."

"This shouldn't take long," he said, a wry smirk curling his lips. "Not if you cooperate."

She failed to see the humor.

"Look, I don't know what you think you saw, but—"

It was his turn to shush her with an upraised palm. "I know you're not FBI," he said.

That puzzled her and her freshly fogged brain tried piecing the situation into something that made sense.

"Care to explain to me why you're questioning my employees?" he said.

Now the pieces came together. "You're in management?"

He nodded. "Gabe Evanski. General Manager." He pushed a hand her way and she shook it. In the process her hand brushed against the cuff of his jacket and she remembered Jack Burrell's earlier comment about a guy in a sharkskin suit. Now, it was her turn, but she'd ended up on the receiving end.

"This is the part where you tell me your name," he said.

"Carolina McKay. No fancy title for me though."

"And the real reason you're here, young lady? Please don't use that line you tried on Randy. He might not be smart enough to know the FBI doesn't have freelancers, but I am."

His words weren't threatening, but she knew better than to feed him a lie.

"Fair enough. But only because you called me young," she said with a smile. "Scarlet is my sister and I'm trying to find out what happened to her."

Gabe cocked his head and she was certain he was going to

have the same reaction as everyone else to that statement. Disbelief. Bewilderment. Instead he nodded. "I can see the resemblance," he said.

"Really?" She tried to decide whether she could believe him.

"There are signs."

"Bullshit," she said.

He chuckled at her change of tone. "I don't want you to get the wrong impression of me. I'm just observant, not a dog like some other characters you encountered here."

"Randy," she said with a quick lift of her brows.

"You said it, not me." He motioned to two plush chairs in the lobby and they both sat. "Your ears, first off. And you have a near identical slope of your nose. Now, I wouldn't have guessed it immediately if you didn't tell me, but once you did, it became obvious."

"Huh," she said, taking zero offense to his assessment.

"Though, your eyes could throw someone off. Not the color, the shape."

"Half-sister," Carolina said.

"Makes sense." The man adjusted himself in the chair. "You got any questions for me?"

"Depends."

"On what?"

"How well you knew my sister."

He nodded. "I don't pretend to know the fine details on all the employees, but I'm confident in the TV Guide version. Scarlet was a good worker, but her head wasn't in this place. I didn't hold that against her. Few shining stars see this kind of job as a long-term solution to life's problems."

"Scarlet was a star?"

Another nod. "Had some of the best people skills I've seen in two decades. And not in a superficial, salesman kind of way. She was genuine and that came through in her dealings with people. I know she didn't have much in the way of an education, but with her personality, she was destined for big things. Bigger than working in the cage, that's for damned sure." He gave a small laugh. "But I'm probably not telling you anything you don't already know."

He was, but she didn't see the sense in telling him that. "Do you think she used those same skills to rob this place?"

Gabe folded and unfolded his hands. "Not for a hot minute. They're looking to pin it on someone and she was an easy target because she stopped coming to work. She's hardly the first to move on to greener pastures without giving two weeks' notice."

"Who's they?"

"The Feds. That fellow in charge of the case, my read on him is that he's the type who looks for simple answers to complicated questions."

It was a pretty thin argument, but something about the way Gabe was so certain, made her believe it, too. Or want to believe it.

"You have any thoughts on who stole the money? If it wasn't my sister?"

Gabe looked past her, into the bowels of the casino. "Pick a card, any card," he said, holding his hand out to the sea of lost souls.

"You seem fond of my sister. Did the two of you ever associate outside of work?"

Gabe flashed a Cheshire cat grin. "Are you asking if we dated?"

"Or more?"

He ran one palm across his slick dome which was buffed to a near mirror finish. "I do believe we played in different leagues, your sister and I. So, no, our relationship was strictly professional."

That sounded truthful enough. "Can I ask you one more question?" she asked.

"Of course."

"You keep referring to Scarlet in the past tense. Why is that?"

His genial smile faltered. "Well, she's an ex-employee. That's why."

That seemed thin too, but she didn't want to put Gabe Evanski on the defensive. At least, not yet.

CHAPTER TEN

Carolina was at the driver's door of her van when she heard Jack's voice behind her.

"Pretty sweet ride," he said.

She turned, not as shocked by his presence as she should have been. "Can't find my sister so now you're stalking me?"

He pulled the lollipop from his mouth, shrugging. "Got bored. Decided to surveil this place for a little while and saw your van. Sort of sticks out." He motioned to the solar panels on the roof and he had a point.

"Well, don't let me keep you," she said, opening the door and climbing into the driver's seat. "The Golden Waters await."

But Jack lingered, his eyes lazily drifting from her to the casino, back and forth. "Find out anything I should know?" he eventually got around to asking.

"If I did you're a pretty shitty agent."

His mouth turned downward as he considered it. "Yeah. I might be."

The man's candor was so surprising that Carolina was speechless, but that didn't last long. "Climb in," she said.

Once inside, Jack ogled her dwelling with too much interest for her comfort. The man just couldn't keep his eyes to himself, but she supposed such habits came with his job.

"I like this," he said, turning back to her. "Saves money on hotels and you don't have to worry about bedbugs. Sort of a home away from home."

"Or just *home*."

He raised an eyebrow. "You live in here?"

"I suppose you could call it that. Sleep when I can, drive when I need to get somewhere. Sometimes I even have a moment to reflect on all my fantastic life choices."

He chuckled, then stopped when he saw she wasn't joking. "You know, it doesn't sound half bad. All that freedom. Not burdened with the baggage of material possessions that accumulate throughout the course of life. Come and go as you please." He nodded as if convincing himself what he said was true. "Yeah. I could appreciate the spartan, nomadic lifestyle."

Carolina swallowed a laugh. "Oh, sure. It's romantic as hell. Just a tip, for when you find yourself rocking out van lifestyle, be on the lookout for those one-week free trial coupons from gyms. Those come in real handy when you can't handle your own stink any longer and need a place to wash up."

He chuckled again... and stopped again. Carolina still wasn't joking.

To change the subject, Jack cleared his throat. "So, I probably shouldn't know any of this, but I take it you went in and talked to the employees?"

She nodded. She knew the family member of a prime suspect insinuating herself into the investigation could cause a shitstorm of epic proportions, but Jack seemed nonplussed.

Maybe he wasn't such a bad guy after all. "A few of them. Then I lost interest."

"Quite the group of winners in there," he said.

Carolina considered it. "Not many I'd want as friends, but nothing unusual."

"Nothing unusual? Jesus, those people are comprised of equal parts desperation, hopelessness, and slime. If that's normal to you, then I have to ask, what type of folks do you associate with?"

She tipped her head his way. "You tell me. You're the one sitting in my van."

"Alright, alright. Bit of a firecracker aren't you?" he asked.

"The big boss. He seemed... knowledgeable," Carolina said.

"Mr. Clean?" Jack asked and she nodded. "Yeah, he's got his finger on things."

"He knew a lot about Scarlet. From the shape of her nose to her career aspirations."

"You think he might have done something to her?" Jack asked.

It was Carolina's turn to shrug. "I don't know. Not really. He sought me out, after all. A guilty person doesn't do that."

"One that's cocky enough might. Could be part of the game to him."

"Maybe." But she wasn't convinced. "What do you think?"

Before Jack could answer, the doors to the casino opened and Randy and Suzette strolled out together. They exchanged a bit of chitchat and then separated in the parking lot.

"Ugh. Those two are the worst of them," Jack said. "She's a Karen on steroids and he's a sleazeball wrapped in flop sweat."

"A Karen?" she asked, watching the two walk through the lot.

"You know, a Karen. 'Let me talk to your manager' and all that jazz." He checked Carolina, but she still had no idea what he was talking about. "Jesus, I'm older than you and I get the internet memes."

Suzette stopped in front of a Subaru hatchback that looked as if it had been rolled down a hill four or five times. The paint had faded to a dishwater gray and the rear windshield was held together with duct tape.

Randy, however, pulled his keys and the lights of a plum crazy purple Dodge Charger flashed twice. It looked fresh off the showroom floor with tires that glistened black and a racing stripe that stretched from the hood to the trunk. With great effort he wedged himself into the vehicle and dropped into the driver's seat. The frame sagged under him as the engine roared like a wildcat in heat.

"Talk about compensating," Carolina said. "What's your take on that one?"

Jack pulled a small notebook from his jacket pocket and flipped a few pages, licking his finger once between. "Randy Drake. Divorced, one kid that lives with his ex in Cleveland."

"Someone not only married him but fucked him?" she asked, remembering all his lecherous leers at anything with two tits.

"For every Adam there's an Eve," Jack said. "But now, this bachelor is back on the market, living with his mother. He has subscriptions to half a dozen different porn sites, most of them fitting into the *barely legal* niche, and he pays to chat with young women in the Ukraine. If that doesn't make you want to swipe right, what will?"

"Swipe right?" she asked. It was like he was speaking a foreign sub-dialect of English which she couldn't decipher. But that wasn't important. "How the hell do you know all that?" she asked him.

"The Patriot Act is an amazing thing."

Carolina shook her head, now he was really pulling her leg. "You're shitting me?"

"It's true. I can get access to what websites you've visited, how long you were on them, what videos you watched, where you paused them. Every email you send and receive. Every search engine query you make. And that's just the tip. Anything you do while connected to the internet, I can find out about it with one phone call. Kinda scary, huh? Glad I'm on this side of the badge."

"Glad I'm not on the internet," she said.

"You're not?" he asked, shock in his voice. "No smartphone?"

She pointed to her burner on the console. "Not even an email address."

"Smart woman," he said.

Randy pulled his Charger from the parking spot and revved the engine, firing it down the lane.

"What do you think mid-level managers make at this place?" she asked.

"I can pull his taxes if you give me a minute."

"How about we trail him instead?"

Jack nodded. "Or that. You drive."

CHAPTER ELEVEN

Carolina kept a moderate distance as she followed Randy Drake, confident that his purple ride would be hard to lose, even as cars weaved in and out between them. They drove for less than two miles before he made a hard right into a Sheetz mini-mart, stopping at a self-serve pump.

"Maybe circle the block," Jack suggested.

Carolina thought that needlessly paranoid. Randy hadn't struck her as the observant type. "Nah," she said. "I don't know the area. About the time I pass by, I'll get stuck on a one-way street and he'll be in the wind before I can backtrack my way out."

She didn't wait for his response to that, pulling into the gas station and stopping at the far end of the parking lot, beside the air pump. Randy already had the nozzle in the Charger, eyes glazed over as he watched the tally grow.

He looked as dim as a dying star and she wondered if she really believed he could have masterminded a casino heist netting hundreds of thousands of dollars, or if she wanted to believe it to clear Scarlet's name.

It struck her how silent the van had become and she turned to Jack to make sure he hadn't dozed off. But he was awake and alert, eyes glued on the man and his sports car. She wouldn't tell him, but she was a little impressed. One minute, he was all jokes, but as soon as the game was on, he was serious, dedicated. Maybe she underestimated him.

She looked past him, back to Randy who was now returning the nozzle to the cradle. When that was done, he pulled a handkerchief from his pocket and used it to wipe away a dribble of spilled gas from the Charger's paint. He shoved the gas-stained rag back into his pocket, then pulled out a cigarette. Yeah, a real mastermind.

Before Randy could light up, a teenage girl in heels and jeans so tight they looked molded to her body passed between Randy and Carolina's rides. His eyes honed in on the girl's ass like it was a beacon flashing *Look at me. Look at me.* His jaw sagged open as he leered.

Then the teen was in the store and Randy's show was over. His head swiveled back, and in the process his eyes met Carolina's. She tried to duck, to sink into the seat, but it was too late. Randy's lecherous gaze became a wide-eyed and knowing stare.

"Shit," she said. "He made us."

"Not us. You. He made you," Jack said, voice gruff. "You're not very good at this, are you?"

Randy forced himself back into the driver's seat of his Charger, not even bothering to close the door to the gas tank, and gunned the engine.

"I'm a little rusty," Carolina said, shifting into drive as Randy was already pulling away from the pump.

Before Carolina could follow, a man hobbling along on a crutch got in the way. Carolina laid on the horn. Startled, he stumbled to the side, barely maintaining his balance.

"Fuck you," the man shouted, holding up two fingers of the middle persuasion.

"Right back at you," Carolina said, hitting the gas.

Randy was already on the road by the time she got out of the parking spot. Traffic was light, but a Port Authority bus cruised along at twenty miles per hour, delaying her exit a good ten seconds. When she finally exited the lot, all she could see of the Charger were taillights.

"Up there," Jack said, pointing.

"I saw him." She shifted again, picking up speed as fast as the van would allow, which wasn't anything to brag about. But, ahead, Randy was stopped at a red light and the momentary delay allowed her to come within five car lengths.

The light flipped green and Randy was on it. His tires spun atop the asphalt with a shrill scream, sending smoke billowing, then caught hold. The Charger took off like it had been shot from a canon.

Carolina floored the gas pedal of her van. The engine revved, but it wasn't the purr of Randy's freshly tuned ride. It was a sick cat hacking up a hairball. The van lurched, bucked, then maxed out just under seventy.

Randy was already half a mile ahead, swerving between cars and trucks like a wannabe Nascar driver. There was no way they would catch him in the van.

"Son of a bitch!" She slammed her hand on the steering wheel.

Jack took the loss easier and yawned. "Can't win 'em all, kid."

"What if he takes off?"

Jack burped out a laugh. "Like what, flee the country? You think that schmoe's gonna catch the red eye to Paris? He doesn't even have a passport." Another yawn, followed by a shake of his head. "He's going home to mommy. Probably has to snag a fresh pair of boxers too."

Carolina breathed deeply, letting her frustration fade. "You're not pissed at me?" she asked.

Jack opened a fresh lollipop. "Not in the slightest. He's spooked. If he's done anything he shouldn't have done, he'll be on edge and that means he'll make a mistake. So while this situation didn't exactly go the way I'd have handled it, I'm sure it'll work out just fine."

Despite her career, despite her accomplishments, it was still reassuring to hear a fellow law enforcement official say you didn't fuck up. "Thanks."

He glanced at her, one eye squinted down with curiosity. "Thanks for what?"

She considered it. "I don't know. It's been a long week." The longest.

"That it has," Jack said. "I think we both need some sleep. Where are you staying, anyway?"

She cocked a thumb toward the van's cargo section where her mattress waited. "You're in it, remember?"

"Oh right," he said, sitting upright after a stretch.

"I'll head back to the casino so you can pick up your rental. Next time we get into a high speed chase, maybe we should take whatever you're driving."

Jack smiled and nodded. "Toyota Corolla. A real Avis special. But, yeah, I bet my per diem it can go faster than your mid-life crisis-mobile."

"I'll pass on that bet," she said.

The city wasn't all bad at night, with the lights reflecting off the black rivers, the bridges glowing golden. There was a kind of charm there, even if she'd rather be parked in the middle of a forest, somewhere far away from people.

"You know, if you want a real bed, I've got a room at the Marriott," Jack said, spoiling the quiet.

She looked at him out of the corner of her eye as she drove. "Is that supposed to be a come on?" she asked.

His cheeks flushed pink. "No, I mean, I, well, I was just trying to be cordial," he stammered.

"That's what they all say," she said. "If you really wanted to get anywhere, you should have led with the shower, not the mattress."

"Well, if you're—"

"Too late, Special Agent," she said, heading back to the casino.

CHAPTER TWELVE

Carolina wrung water from her hair as she stepped out of the steaming shower, her feet slick against the tile floor. She wiped her hand over the fogged mirror, creating a clear spot for her face to show through, then cracked the bathroom door open to create an escape point for the hot air.

She'd planned to sleep in the van. It was what she was used to, after all. But after Jack's failed come on, she had an epiphany. Why sleep in her vehicle, parked on some random side street, when her sister's luxurious apartment was sitting empty? She was a lot of things, but wasteful was not one of them.

Once some of the steam subsided, she was able to get a better view of herself. The paramedic had done a good job of stitching the stab wound on her arm closed. There was no redness—a good sign—and the cut was clean.

It would leave a scar, but she had others, most worse. There was a football-sized bruise on her side, beneath which broken ribs screamed every time she took too deep a breath. Which reminded her...

Two Percocets, down the hatch. She yearned for a third but had to ration them, at least until she could get a prescription for Oxy. Conning that out of one of her doctors was going to be her first mission of the day.

The deep purple bruises on her face had already begun to yellow. Scarlet had a stash of makeup that would make a cosmetologist jealous and even though Carolina wasn't skilled at the application process, she was relatively confident she'd be able to cover them well enough to avoid too many stares.

All things considered, she was in tip-top shape. For her anyway. Even if that was a low bar.

Less than a minute into applying foundation, her phone buzzed on the sink, the vibrations fluttering it off the rim and into the bowl where remnants of used toothpaste spit lingered. Carolina grabbed it, wiped it clean on a towel, and looked at the number.

She expected it to be Bea, desperate for an update, for news. For good news.

She'd already decided she wasn't going to answer, then she saw the number and recognized it as the one Jack had given her the night prior.

"What do you want?" she asked, pulling the towel up to cover her exposed chest as if he could somehow see her breasts through the connection.

"Well, good morning to you too. How's life in Le Case de Vana?" Jack asked and from his voice she could tell he was grinning as he said it.

"Just fine." He didn't need to know.

"Not a morning person, huh? I should have guessed. Anyway, I have something that might wipe that sour expression off your face."

She looked at herself in the mirror. She was scowling. Then she looked at the phone, the thirty dollar burner she replaced every month or two. There was a terrible camera on the phone, but no way to video chat, so he couldn't actually see her. Could he?

His braggadocio over all the info he could mine regarding internet habits had her wary. She was going to need to stick a piece of masking tape across that camera, just in case. In the meantime, she covered it with her finger.

"Screw off," she said, cheerful as ever.

"Jesus. Get yourself some coffee. Then meet me at eighteen fifty-five East Franklin Street."

"Why?" she asked.

"Can't say. It'll ruin the surprise."

She looked back to her face, then the makeup at the vanity. "Give me thirty minutes."

"Be there in fifteen. Otherwise you might miss all the fun."

CHAPTER THIRTEEN

FLASHING LIGHTS AHEAD CAUGHT HER ATTENTION AS SHE rolled up East Franklin. Pittsburgh City Police cars littered the street and enough uniformed officers lined the street that it looked like half-price day at the all-you-can-eat buffet.

"What the fuck are you up to, Jack?" she asked herself as she pulled into a parking spot parallel to the street.

According to her GPS she was still a hundred or so yards away from the address Jack had given her, but the road from here on out was blocked. Residents hovered in their small yards, heads craned in the direction of the commotion. Everyone was so caught up in the commotion that no one paid her any attention as she hurried along the sidewalk. That suited her just fine.

As she neared the cops, she spotted Jack sitting on the hood of his rented Toyota, a cell phone pressed against his ear. He hadn't seen her yet, but she quickened her pace to a slow jog. No officers stopped her and she was relieved there was no crime scene tape to hop. After all, this wasn't Dupray where she had friends in high places.

"What the hell is going on?" Carolina asked, sidling up next to Jack who only at that moment became aware of her presence.

He held up a slender index finger. Wait. Then spoke into the phone. "Yeah, it's going down right now. I'll call as soon as we wrap up. You too."

He pocketed his phone, then stared at her long enough for it to be awkward.

"What?" she asked, her stomach tightening. That was the kind of long pause people took before dealing bad news.

"Something a little different today." He gave a genuine smile and almost looked handsome. "You look good without all the bruises."

She frowned. Did she put the makeup on to be noticed, or to not be noticed? The extra attention made her uncomfortable. If she hadn't been so focused on the throng of police and whatever was about to go down, she would have retorted with something about looking good enough for him to hit on her yesterday. Oh well, life moves on.

Instead, she settled on, "Fuck off."

That only made his smile grow even wider. "You say the sweetest things to me."

Carolina didn't mind the banter, but the nagging question still hung in the air.

"Tell me what's happening," she said.

Jack nodded. "Oh yeah, that. I thought you were gonna miss it." He pointed to a plain, two-story house where the front door hung ajar, uniformed officers manning each side of the frame. "Keep your eyes on the prize," he said, his own eyes glued to the doorway. He sounded giddy as a schoolboy.

Carolina followed his gaze and within seconds, it happened.

Randy Drake was led through the doorway by a buff Pittsburgh cop. His hands were cuffed behind him and he wore nothing but dingy, white briefs. His gut hung low over the waistband and she noticed holes in the elastic around his thighs, holes through which pubic hair poked. She shuddered at the sight and was glad she skipped breakfast.

Randy was bawling, snot dripping from his nose and getting caught in his wild rug of chest hair. "I'm sorry, mama, I'm sorry!" he blathered. The buff cop, whose biceps looked as big around as milk jugs, shoved him down the walkway toward an awaiting squad car.

Through his sobbing and tears, Randy saw her and Jack watching this all go down. He summoned whatever fight he had left in him and struggled against the cop's powerful grip, straining to get at them.

"You cocksuckers!" Randy yelled, but the cop reigned him in, giving his cuffed wrists a hard yank that had the man crying again. As he passed by Carolina and Jack he worked up a mouthful of spit and launched it at them. It landed a good two feet short.

"I wouldn't even give that an A for effort," Carolina said and, with that, Randy was being shoved into the back seat of the cruiser.

"Spill it," Carolina said to Jack.

Jack grinned. "Ocean's Eleven here made a deposit of two hundred thousand dollars into mama's, I mean, Nanette's personal checking account last night. Pair that up with the brand-new Dodge Charger..." He made a tsk, tsk sound with his tongue. "I bet it takes less than fifteen minutes before he cracks and confesses."

Then shouts of, "Don't you hurt my boy!" drowned out everything else.

Both Carolina and Jack looked to the house where a woman burst outside, her hands balled into fists. "You lay a hand on my boy and I'll have your badges!"

Carolina knew this was the aforementioned Mama aka

Nanette. She was in her sixties, clad in pajamas, her hair in curlers.

Jack laughed without candor. "Oh man, this might actually make up for being transferred to financial crimes."

She looked at him, wondering what the hell that meant. But it didn't matter. She had other, more important questions.

"If Randy's your thief, then what's going on with my sister?"

Some of the triumphant glee left Jack's face. He gave a quick shrug of his shoulders. "No idea. But the FBI no longer considers her a suspect."

Carolina had almost begun to like the man, but his cavalier attitude erased that. "That's it? No longer a suspect? So, what, you're just going to ride back to DC on your high horse caring fuck all about my missing sister?"

Now all his good cheer was gone and his mustache twitched. "Sorry, Carolina, but I have no jurisdiction. It's in the hands of the local PD's deal now."

She stepped away from him. "Thanks for nothing, Jack. You really are a shitty agent."

He moved away from her, toward the cops. "Never said I wasn't."

Carolina wasn't going to get anything else from him. He was another stuffed suit, capable of doing the easy work, but unwilling to get his hands dirty. She wanted to call him out in public, in front of this sea of real cops, but knew it would do no good aside from letting her blow off steam.

Instead she turned to the police car where Randy Drake openly wept in the back seat. She pushed toward him, ignoring the questioning looks from police, putting a shoulder into his mother to get her out of the way. She was a woman on a mission.

"Where's my sister, Randy?" Carolina demanded.

Randy stared at her through bloodshot, bleary eyes. "Your sister? What?" he asked, clueless.

"Scarlet. Did she catch you stealing the money?" She grabbed a fistful of his greasy hair. "Did you do something to her?"

The buff policeman had her by the shoulders. "Please, ma'am, step away from the suspect."

"Get that bitch off from my boy!" Nanette shouted from the sidelines. "He's got rights!"

Carolina ignored them both. "If you hurt her I swear to God I'll find out!"

Randy sobbed. Nanette screamed. And then Carolina felt herself being lifted off the ground, pain shrieking in her wrecked shoulder.

Buff cop carried her away from the car, putting her down on the sidewalk like an unruly toddler in time out. He stared at her with icy, blue eyes. "Do I need to arrest you too?" he asked, his voice thick with a nasally Pittsburgh accent.

She took a deep breath, trying to calm herself but it didn't do much good. What she needed was a pill, chewed not swallowed this time. "No," she said to the cop. "I'll go."

He tipped his head in a skeptical nod and felt his eyes stay on her as she left the scene. As soon as she was apart from curious onlookers she grabbed the stolen pill bottle from her pocket and extracted a Percocet. She didn't have anything to wash the bitter taste off her tongue after chewing it into a paste, but that was okay. It hit fast and her temper faded concurrently.

She threw a glance back to the scene. Did she really think Randy Drake could be responsible for Scarlet's disappearance? The odds were slim, but what else did she have to go on?

She was back where she started and the question was the same.

Where the hell was her sister?

CHAPTER FOURTEEN

SHE WAS BACK IN SCARLET'S BEDROOM, THE PLACE WHERE women kept their secrets. As she searched through a dresser, she found nothing of importance. Clothes, clothes, and more clothes. The vast majority of them seemed to be undergarments—bras, panties, teddies. Corsets with so many straps and loops you needed to be a puzzle master to put them on.

Carolina had never been the girliest of girls, but she was no prude. Yet she couldn't fathom why one person would need so much lingerie.

Her hand hit the bottom of the drawer much sooner than she would have thought. She extracted armfuls of delicates, tossing them onto the bed in order to explore further.

It was just what she thought. The dovetail joints continued down the side, but didn't align with the bottom. There was a hidden compartment.

As Carolina flipped the drawer upside down, a thin slab of birch tumbled out, gouging the hardwood floor. Whoops. She'd just pretend that divot was there when she arrived.

The other object that fell free was a hot pink leather case

holding an iPad. Aside from that, the compartment was empty, meaning the iPad must be important enough to hide, and not due to the cost. If Scarlet could afford this apartment, this view, these clothes, a seven hundred dollar iPad wasn't going to break her. This tablet was hidden because it contained something her sister wanted—or needed—to keep secret.

Carolina flipped open the case, her finger dropping to the wake button. She doubted it would work. If it had been sitting in the drawer for a week or more the charge was probably drained, but it was worth a try.

The screen remained black. She then remembered the power button. Maybe Scarlet was one of those rare birds that actually powered down their tablets to conserve on the battery. She held it in and a moment later the screen brightened to life.

"Yes!" she said to herself, triumphant.

Then the keypad popped up. Password required.

"Shit."

She wondered what combination her sister might use. First she plugged in Scarlet's birthday. At least, she hoped it was Scarlet's birthday. Either way, it didn't work. She tried Bea's. Nothing.

She cocked her head as an idea came to her. What about her own birthday? It's something no intruder would know. Something that may as well be random. It might just work.

Only it didn't.

"Motherfucker."

The next message informed her there were too many incorrect attempts and that she was locked out temporarily. A timer counted down the minutes until she could try again. But trying again was pointless. She'd never outguess the password on her own. Good thing she had her own computer expert on standby.

CHAPTER FIFTEEN

Max Barrasso gawked at the room, the furniture, the artwork on the walls. He seemed in shock or awe or both.

"Damn." The word came out in two long syllables. "This looks like something out of Long & Foster. What the hell does your sister do anyway?"

"Half-sister," Carolina said. There it was again. Covering up for lack of knowledge. "And she works at a casino."

"As what, the CEO? Because ain't no one dealing cards or spinning the roulette wheel that can afford this kind of lifestyle."

"That's half the reason you're here," Carolina said. "Because none of this makes sense."

When she'd called him the day before, she thought she might be able to plug the iPad into a computer or something and he could hack it long distance. That made him laugh and laugh. Once he explained he needed the iPad to do what she needed, she'd offered to overnight it to him in New York. Instead, he said he'd come to her.

That the man was willing to make a six-hour drive for her

without asking questions and with no strings attached, touched a piece of her heart she wasn't sure even existed anymore.

"I still can't believe you came," she said, taking in his dark, striking features. He'd let his hair grow out more since she's last seen him, something akin to a mini afro now topping his head. But the smile, the eyes, were the same. Warm and kind.

"Shit," he said. "I can't leave my number one girl in a lurch. Besides, maybe you'll stumble into something big again. Give me the scoop. Remember what a great team we make?"

She'd forgotten how grandiose he could be and some of the cheer at seeing him began to fade. "Yeah, a real Starsky and Hutch." She grabbed the iPad off the kitchen island, extending it to him. "At least now you can actually help me with something."

He opened his arms out to her with his gleaming smile still plastered on his face. "Carolina McKay, it's good to see you, too." He went in for a hug. She pushed the iPad into his hands.

Sighing, Max slid the messenger bag off his shoulder and set it on the island. He withdrew a laptop, silver with the bitten apple on the case. Without a word, he pulled out some cables and connected his laptop to the tablet, typing away on his own machine.

"What are you doing?" Carolina asked.

He kept his eyes locked on his screen when he talked. "Are you looking for a real explanation, or just trying to fill the awkward silence? Cause if you want a lesson in hacking, or at the very least, how computers and software works, I don't even know where to begin with a troglodyte like you."

Carolina nodded, understanding that it was better to just let the man work and not ask pointless questions. She was good at a lot of things, but anything computer related wasn't on that list and she didn't have any desire to remedy that.

She sat across from him, sipping some designer brand of

coffee she'd found in Scarlet's cabinet from her Charm City mug. But Max was right. She didn't like the awkward silence.

"I was getting bored waiting for you and thought I might take it to one of those pretentious Apple stores. Have one of the techies there help me out instead, but I didn't want to wound your ego."

"Ha!" Max barked out. "Those neckbeards would have reported it stolen."

"I'm her sister," she said.

"Half," Max stressed the word. "Sister." He checked her out, making no attempt to conceal his staring. "No offense, but you look even worse than the last time I saw you. Do you like, get the shit beat out of you for fun? Is that your hobby? Because, if it is, find a new one."

Carolina felt herself folding inward, trying to cover up her injuries and wounds. Max must have noticed and went serious. "I'm just giving you shit because I care about you. I know what you've been through the last few weeks. And it's okay to take a break sometimes, you know?"

She finished off her coffee in a long, scalding swallow. "I planned to, but what can I say? Scarlet picked a piss poor time to disappear."

Max nodded. "Preach it."

A few more keystrokes and he lifted his hands from the keyboard. He blew on his fingers like they were too hot to handle, then slid the tablet to Carolina.

"Seriously?" she asked. "That's all there was to it?"

"What you just witnessed was fine art. Skills honed over countless hours of practice and hard work. Hacking one of those bastards if like playing Partita Number Two in D Minor on the violin."

She stared at him for a second, again amazed at his seemingly bottomless layers, then turned her attention to the iPad. The digital keypad was gone, replaced with the unlock slider at the bottom of the screen. She swiped it to the side and the black screen turned to a colorful desktop full of different apps.

"Holy shit, you really did it," she said.

"Your skepticism hurts my heart." Max interlaced his fingers then bent them backward, snapping his knuckles rapid fire. "I had to pinpoint the last time she used it, then dive into DFU mode and—"

"No lessons, remember?" She was already checking the apps, seeing what all there was to explore.

"So I guess that's it, then. Wham, bam, and not even a thank you ma'am, huh? You always make me feel so used," he said.

"Shove it." She clicked on the apps that were self-explanatory. The address book was empty, no entries at all not even Bea. Or Carolina, but that was no shock. Next she tried pictures, of which there were plenty. But they were all places. Mountain views. The deck of a yacht. A beach pressed against brilliant blue water. No places. No photos of Scarlet or her friends.

Frustrated, she turned to Max. "Don't people usually have pictures of themselves on these things?" she asked.

"Pictures of themselves," Max parroted. "Like selfies?"

His grin was nauseating and he must have seen she wasn't amused.

"How old is she?" he asked.

"Late twenties."

"Jesus, Carolina. You don't even know her exact age?"

She thought about it, trying to go off her own age and work backward. "Twenty eight. I think. Or nine. And I can do without the guilt trip."

Max rolled his eyes. "Sure. But yeah, that's a pretty good age for the selfie crowd. You sure there aren't any? Did you check the cloud?"

Her hesitation gave him all the info he needed and he pulled one of the stools around the island and sidled up next to her. She put the iPad between them, in neural ground. Then he tapped an icon.

More vacation-type photos loaded. "Nothing there," Max said, then returned to the home screen. "No Instagram or Snapchat either." He checked Carolina, curious.

"I know what those are," she said. "You don't have to explain it."

"Alright. I'm just checking. Don't want to leave you in the dust here." He went back to the screen, swiping to the next page which was only a third full. Then his shoulder sagged and some of his abundance of confidence left him. "Maybe I drove all the way here for nothing," he said and he sounded so disappointed she almost felt bad for him.

"It's okay." But it wasn't. This was her last lead. She'd ransacked the apartment and found nothing that gave a hint to Scarlet's life or associated. It was a beautiful, blank slate. Just like Scarlet herself.

"I just can't believe..." Max's voice trailed off as he rechecked the apps. He tapped a folder which opened to emptiness, but paused. "Hold up," he said.

He swiped upward, again and again and again, and then another folder appeared. Underneath it read **NSA ADS**. He paused before opening it.

"She had this hidden," he said, stating the obvious. "Are you okay if it's like some weird shit?"

"How weird can it be?" Carolina asked, then she tapped the folder herself.

Max stared at the tablet, wary as the folder loaded. "You'd be surprised."

It opened to endless rows of photographs. And these images were of Scarlet. There were dozens, maybe a hundred and in all of them she was dressed in only the kinds of lingerie Carolina had found in her closet and drawers.

In many, she wasn't dressed at all. These photos weren't selfies either. They were professionally shot with perfect lighting, exquisite posing. Her little sister looked like a Victoria's Secret model.

Max's eyes seemed ready to pop free from their sockets. "Damn. Is that Scarlet?" he asked.

"Yeah." The word came out in a whisper because she knew what these photos were. Despite their high quality, they weren't modeling shots. And they weren't meant for a portfolio. These images weren't created to sell lingerie. Their purpose was selling the person wearing it.

Everything began to click. Scarlet refusing to work nights and weekends at the casino. Her absurd amount of sexy-time outfits. Her lifestyle.

"Let me see that," Max said, reaching for the tablet and double-tapping one of the more risqué shots to enlarge it.

In that photo, Scarlet was completely naked, sprawled on her back. Her blonde hair was perfectly messy, strewn across a pillow.

"Don't be a pervert," Carolina said, trying to turn the iPad away from him.

"I'm not. Really. Look." He worked his fingers to zoom in, not on Scarlet's naughty bits, but on an index card lying on the bed beside her. Written on it was a phone number. "Is that Scarlet's number?"

"No. Not the one my mom has, anyway."

Max pulled out his phone.

"What are you doing?" she asked.

"Calling the number. Seems logical, right?"

He had a point. He put the phone on speaker and they listened to it ring five times before going to a generic, automated voicemail.

"Mailbox full. Goodbye," the computerized voice said after asking them to leave a message.

"Plan B, uh, no pun intended," Max said, catching a glare from Carolina.

He switched to texting. In the To field he typed the number in the photograph, then typed:

R U available? I have $$$$

"Now what?" Carolina asked.

"We wait," Max said.

And they did.

CHAPTER SIXTEEN

It was dark and humid in the barn. The air felt heavy enough to hold her down. She'd been there for days, maybe even a week. As one sunset faded in the next it was hard to keep count.

She shifted her weight and the chain attached to her leg clanged against itself. The noise was like an explosion in the relative silence and she froze, body tense. Then it dawned that the sound had come from her. Not him.

She breathed again.

Did anyone miss her? Her mother might, but what about the people who saw her day to day? Her coworkers. Her clients. Was anyone looking for her or had they moved on to some new girl? Someone who wasn't ignoring their calls and texts.

Would she ever be found?

She could hear animals outside the barn, snorting, squawking, making their presence known. Not that they could help her.

Moonlight spilled through an irregular hole in the ceiling, painting an oblong circle in the straw a few yards from where she was confined. In the wall behind her, the barn siding fit together poorly, allowing a sliver of illumination. During the days she stared through that quarter inch gap, trying to see someone that could help her. But all she spied with her little eye was the occasional hog or hen.

They didn't help.

As she pushed herself into a sitting position, the lower half of her body screamed. Her thighs were purple and black bruises. The cuff on her foot had cut so deep that she could see what she assumed to be raw muscle through the wound. Those injuries were mostly from fighting and from struggling. Inflicted as she tried to keep him from taking what he so desired. From what she didn't want to give to him.

But he took it anyway.

Blood seeped from her groin, reminding her that she was no match for him. That he could take whatever he wanted whenever he wanted it. There was no end. No out. No escape.

Across from her, in another stall, laid Eve. She'd been there when Scarlet arrived, chained and beaten and bleeding. A sign of things to come.

When he wasn't around, the women talked. Eve thought she'd been there for two weeks, but much of the time the words she said made little sense. She rambled when she spoke, which was infrequent. Most of the time she just laid there, so silent Scarlet thought she was dead or dying.

Eve wished she was though. She'd told Scarlet that in fleeting moments of coherence.

"I can't take any more," Eve had said, in her raspy, barely there voice. "I want to die."

Scarlet tried to be encouraging, to promise hope and salvation. Even only a few days in, she doubted such vows would ever come to realization, but it seemed like the kind of thing you just did. Life's most important pep talks.

Eve hadn't responded. And when he came in later that day

to force himself on the woman, Eve didn't struggle. She laid on the dirt floor and took what he gave her, her body limp as a rag, her eyes vacant. Her mind gone.

She hadn't spoken since then, no matter how often Scarlet had tried to cajole conversation from her. She was a body going through the mechanics of living, but what made her human was somewhere far, far away.

Maybe Eve has the right idea, Scarlet thought. Maybe it's better to give up and check out. After all, how much could a person really take before they're broken beyond repair?

So, even though Scarlet wasn't alone, she was. Trapped in this barn with nothing but her own thoughts which grew darker with each passing hour. With the knowledge that he'd soon return with his insatiable appetite.

That happened an hour later. She'd managed to fall asleep only to be woken by the metallic grinding of the barn door sliding along its track. Her body tensed as she waited for his footsteps to approach.

Soon enough, they came.

Scarlet looked to where Eve was sprawled on her side, face in a pile of moldy straw. The woman was breathing, but she didn't react.

Scarlet strained to see beyond the man as he entered the barn but all that laid behind him was a stygian, featureless landscape. No way of knowing where she was, or how to flee.

With nothing to see but the monster who held her captive, she retreated into her own stall, pressing her back against the barn wall. She pulled her knees tight to her chest and tried to stop shaking. That was a losing battle.

Scarlet hid in the hopes that he wouldn't turn to her first. She hated herself for it, for leaving the burden all on Eve, but she knew the woman was already gone. And she didn't want to end up like her.

The man walked, bowlegged and awkward, more of a lope

than a stride. He stopped between the two stalls where that irregular beam of moonlight illuminated him in a way that made Scarlet think of a Broadway star performing in the spotlight. But this man was no star. He was a nightmare. He was horror. He was evil upright.

His long, greasy hair hung in strings across his pinched, ratty face, but his beady eyes peered through the strands, like a man peeking through tall grass. His teeth were jagged and broken, some turned sideways, one growing through the front of the gum at an angle that made it visible even when his mouth was closed.

He was small, maybe five and a half feet, and lean, but strong. So goddamn strong. He could pick either of the women up like they were sacks of flour and when his hand squeezed, his grip felt strong enough to break bones.

Maybe even worse than the sight of him was his aroma. It was a rotting, fetid smell, like soft cheese left unrefrigerated on a hot day. Then there was the pungent, sour fragrance that emanated from his crotch. So far as she could tell from their much too close encounters, he'd never wiped his ass in all his life, and the skin down there was chapped and riddled with festering sores.

Don't pick me tonight, she thought, her self-loathing strong.

He tilted his head back, filthy hair tumbling from his face, and aimed his nose skyward. He sniffed like a hound on the trail of a rabbit, inhaling several deep breaths. Then his tongue, that gray hunk of meat he liked to lick them with, poked free of his mouth and skittered across his lips.

Another sniff. Then he turned.

To Eve.

Scarlet felt the breath she wasn't even aware she was holding leave her in a quick woosh. How can I be such a terrible person, she wondered. She'd made mistakes in her life. She's sold her body to the highest bidders. She's allowed herself to be used. But she'd never hurt other people, until now.

The man stomped toward Eve, halving the distance. Scarlet tried to open her mouth, to say something that would reach him, that would make him react like a human being instead of this thing, but she was frozen.

He knelt beside Eve, his flannel shirt riding up in the back and revealing the gun he always carried in the small of his back. Then he reached out forcing two fingers into the limp woman's mouth. As he lifted her head out of the straw she remained a rag doll.

Scarlet pushed herself away from the wall, forcing herself to get closer to them. And she made herself speak.

"Leave her alone tonight!" She tried to shout the words but they came out little more than a whisper. It was enough to get his attention.

He turned away from Eve, staring at Scarlet, something akin to confusion on his dim face.

"Do whatever you want to me instead," she said.

She didn't want it, not at all, but she couldn't sit there and watch Eve take any more pain.

The man frowned, his pointy nose wrinkling. "You don't boss me," he said. The words were guttural, barely words at all.

He dropped Eve's face, her head smacking against the wood floor, then he went to Scarlet.

She felt her stomach tighten, her body freeze. She wasn't ready for this. Not again. Never again.

When he got close enough, he kicked out with a heavy work boot, the steel toe catching her in the knee. She tumbled sideways, smacking against the stall wall. Only willpower kept her from sobbing.

Then, to her shock, he turned away. Scarlet clawed at him, her hands catching the leg of his jeans, the same pants he'd been wearing the entire time she was here. The same jeans he'd been wearing for years maybe.

"No," Scarlet said.

But he shook her free, then stomped her hand. The sound of phalanges breaking reverberated through her ears, bringing with it a new, exquisite level of pain. She recoiled, huddling against the wall where she had a front row seat for what was about to occur. As much as she didn't want to see it, she couldn't look away.

He grabbed Eve by the hair, raising her upper body off the ground. A soft groan slipped from the woman's mouth, but her eyes remained closed, her body limp. He pulled her face close into his own, so tight their noses smashed together.

"Play!" he grunted.

No response.

He forced his tongue into her mouth, head thrashing side to side in some horrible combination of kissing and biting and chewing. When he pulled back both their mouths were bloody.

Eve remained vacant.

"You're no fun anymore," he said, then released her hair. She landed in a heap. If not for the slow, rhythmic rise and fall of her chest, Scarlet would have thought she was dead.

The man reached behind his back and pulled out the gun, but once it was free of his belt, Scarlet realized it wasn't a gun, not in the traditional sense. It looked rudimentary, yet futuristic at the same time. Like a child's drawing of a gun brought to life.

Maybe he made this thing, Scarlet thought. He could have carved it from wood, painted it black. Maybe this weapon which had kept them so fearful was harmless.

She was wrong, though.

It looked odd because it wasn't an ordinary firearm. It was a captive bolt pistol, the kind used to put down livestock.

The man knew how to use it. He had plenty of experience.

He pressed the barrel of the pistol tight against Eve's

forehead, then paused, maybe to see if this would finally get the reaction he wanted. To see if she was playing possum. But Eve's mind was gone and it wasn't coming back now or ever.

It was time for her body to catch up.

The man pulled the trigger. The noise wasn't like a gunshot, it was a burst of air combined with an explosion.

A small spray of blood backfired into his face as Eve's head snapped away. A dime-sized hole between her eyes leaked blood.

It was finally over. For her.

But Scarlet remained. Now she was alone. The only focus for his urges, his violence. His only toy.

She screamed.

The man paid her no attention. He hoisted Eve's now limp body over his shoulder and turned around, leaving Scarlet sobbing in the dark.

She heard him make his pig call. It wasn't the sue-y sound people made in movies though. It was a grunting, moaning howl. It sounded almost mournful. Wild. Bestial. And it brought the hogs running.

CHAPTER SEVENTEEN

"I don't understand how this works," Carolina said, riding in the passenger seat of Max's rental. It was a Prius, and as much as it reeked of pretension, she had to admit that it was a smoother ride than her van provided.

"We can use the iPad to locate her iPhone. They're linked. It's a tracker, of sorts," Max said, glancing her way. "Are you really this clueless? You aren't even that old. Shit, my grandma knows this."

"Thanks for that," she said, not enjoying being schooled by a man more than a decade her junior. "Sounds a little too big brother for me."

"Time to get with the times, Carolina. Sacrifice some liberties for the sake of convenience," Max said.

She hoped he was joking, but she knew that it wasn't actually far off from reality. It seemed like these days, nobody worried about privacy unless it suited some political agenda. They'd happily accept a tracking chip as long as they could FaceTime on the toilet. Idiots.

"We follow that little dot on the screen," Max said. "It's like the X on a treasure map."

God, he's explaining it to me like I'm five, Carolina thought. She nodded, not wanting to add anything more, lest she be again ridiculed for her lack of technological know-how.

They'd been driving for fifteen or so minutes, weaving through the city. They'd started out in Pittsburgh's version of Beverly Hills but the more they drove, the worse the surroundings became. By this point they were in a section of town where every third building was deserted and boarded up, every business was behind a barbed wire fence, and every person on the street looked at the out of place Prius with a mixture of distrust and disdain.

"We should have taken my van," Carolina said.

Max laughed, then looked to Carolina. "Oh, you were serious. What's that thing get, eight miles to the gallon? My conscience couldn't handle that."

She hated sitting in the passenger seat. She wanted to drive, to be in control of where they were going and how they got there. She didn't like being along for someone else's ride, even if it was Max.

"You see how everyone looks at us?"

He nodded. "Like we're narcs. That's alright. Keep 'em on their toes."

"Unless they decide to unload a magazine into this tin can."

He opened his mouth to respond, then stopped as something changed on the iPad screen. "It's in here," Max said, turning into a complex which was clearly public housing, the kind built in the seventies and not updated since then.

After parking, they both exited the vehicle, Max carrying the iPad as he took in their surroundings. "Not much to look at."

He was right. The brick facades were cracked and crumbling. Many of the windows had strips of tape holding the glass together. Bedsheets and towels served as curtains. The sidewalks pitched and yawed as tree roots threw them out of level.

"Good thing we're not looking to rent," Carolina said, staring at the dot on the tablet as it grew nearer.

After a few turns, they were almost there. It took ascending one cramped stairwell, then Max assured her they'd arrived.

She knocked on the door to apartment 1740, a slab of maroon steel marred with numerous dents and rust spots. Her hand fell to the grip of her revolver, a habit she seemed destined to never shake.

"Maybe hold up on the Annie Oakley shit," Max whispered.

He was right of course. She covered the gun with her jacket, but felt better knowing it was there.

Inside came footsteps, then several clicks and clacks as a series of locks were freed. And then the door opened a few inches.

The face of a thin dark man with a carefully trimmed beard peered at them with wide, untrusting eyes. "Yes?" he asked in an accent that Carolina couldn't place.

"I have a few questions for you," Carolina said.

The man looked terrified but she couldn't tell if it was out of guilt or the more general fear of outsiders. "What about? I know nothing of whatever it is you are inquiring."

"If you don't know why we're here, how do you know you know nothing?" she asked, already annoyed with him. Why couldn't people just be honest?

He tried to shut the door, but Carolina was ahead of him. She shoved her foot in the jamb, making sure it couldn't close, then thrust the door inward, pushing the man with it.

"Carolina," Max hissed. "Calm down."

She let herself inside, head on a swivel as she scanned the place for potential dangers, finding none. To call it cramped was an understatement. The living room was attached to the kitchen and the two combined didn't top two hundred square feet. A small flat screen was balanced on a TV tray. A worn-out couch was the only seating. Through two open doors she could see the lone bedroom and bath. The place made her van look like a palace and it smelled like a mixture of curry and cumin.

The man pressed himself into the wall, trying to disappear into it. Beside him was a lone photograph, no bigger than a credit card. It showed this man standing beside a woman who was holding a newborn baby.

"I haven't done anything wrong, you can't treat me like this," the man pleaded.

Max grabbed Carolina by the shoulder and looked her in the eye. "Stop it," he said.

She clenched her teeth and took a deep breath, trying to douse the fire inside. "My sister's life might be in danger," she whispered to him. "And this schmuck has her phone."

"I'll handle it," Max said. "You stand here and chill."

She hated taking orders, but another look at the trembling man proved her way wasn't working. "Go ahead."

Max stepped between the two of them, putting on his thousand dollar grin. He extended his hand to the man who stared at it like he expected it to bite him.

"I'm Max. This is my friend, Carolina. And no, you haven't done anything wrong. We're looking for someone though, and our search brought us here. Can I ask your name, sir?"

"Siraji Amiri," he said. "Are you here to deport me? I have my papers. I can get them for you. They're in the bedroom."

He took a step in that direction, but Max held up his hand in a stop gesture and the man obeyed.

"No, sir. We're not with immigration. We're looking for a woman. Maybe you've seen her. White. Blonde hair, late twenties, looks like she could squeeze her waist through a keyhole."

Carolina shot a glare to Max. She was sure he caught it, though he did a good job of ignoring her.

Siraji shook his head. "No, nobody like that."

"You're sure?" Max asked.

The man nodded, head bobbing, frantic.

Carolina had drifted deeper in the apartment, toward the couch. She saw a shard of pink between the couch cushions and dug in for it. It was an iPhone in a pink, rhinestone accented case.

"I wouldn't have pegged pink as your favorite color," she said to Siraji.

"It came with the phone. I just bought it three days ago. It cost me a lot of money, but I needed one for my job."

"And what job would that be?" Carolina asked.

"I buy and and sell goods. It's easier with a camera phone."

"Goods, like drugs?" Carolina asked, but even as she asked the question she hated herself for it.

Siraji shook his head again. "Come," he said and they followed him to the bedroom.

On the floor a pile of merchandise was strewn. Sporting goods, secondhand clothing, trinkets, home decor.

"You're like, a flipper?" Max asked. "You buy stuff cheap, add on a couple bucks, and resell?"

The man nodded.

"That's a good hustle, my man." Max held out his hand again, this time in a fist, and to Carolina's surprise, Siraji fist bumped him back.

Carolina had little interest in their bonding moment. She waved the phone in front of her. "This belongs to my sister."

"I didn't know. I paid for it, I promise."

"Who'd you buy it from?"

"I got it at the pawn store. Downtown Pawn, on Cochran."

A crib sat in the corner of the room, pushed tight against the double bed. In it, a baby began to cry.

"May I?" Siraji asked.

Carolina motioned for him to go ahead and the man went to the crib, picking up a baby girl who couldn't be more than five months old. He rocked her in his arms, gentle, caring. "I know nothing of your sister, I promise."

She knew Siraji was telling the truth, but she wasn't happy about it. "What's her name?" she asked.

"Mucjiso," he said. "It means miracle."

As he rocked the girl, her crying slowed, then stopped altogether. Carolina realized Max was staring at her and she could read his expression. It was time to go.

She nodded in agreeance.

"Thank you for your help, Siraji," Max said.

"You're very welcome." Then, he looked at Carolina. "Would you like to keep the phone?" he asked her.

Her eyes drifted around the room, the few ragged belongings of this poor family. Then she pushed it toward him. "You paid for it. And I doubt my sister needs it anymore."

CHAPTER EIGHTEEN

AN OPPRESSIVE SIGN THAT SAID CHECK CASHING & PAYDAY LOANS was plastered on the side of the building and they both missed the much smaller one reading DOWNTOWN PAWN until their second trip around the block. The latter was there almost as an afterthought, some lame attempt at scrounging a few more nickels from their broke clientele.

Inside, the bulk of the lobby was focused on a rope line leading toward counters that had bulletproof glass surrounding them. Tucked far in the rear was a small area of used electronics, jewelry, coins, and junk store level collectibles.

Business was far from booming. Three people were lined up behind the booth for check cashing and one at the payday loans counter. An elderly woman in a Christmas tree sweater browsed the goods.

Aside from the tellers, the only employee was a middle-aged woman who seemed more concerned with playing mahjong on her cell phone than customer service. Carolina stood in front of her for exactly three seconds before sighing in audible annoyance.

"It's a great day at Downtown Check Cashing and Pawn," she said without looking up. "How can I help you?"

"I need some information on a stolen phone which was purchased here."

That got her attention. The woman looked up revealing thick glasses and a pair of eyebrows in desperate need of a wax. "You the cops?"

"We are," Carolina lied.

The woman looked closer and her eyes narrowed. Carolina knew she'd seen her bruises through the makeup. "Bullshit. Get outta here."

Carolina stepped closer, invading the woman's personal space. "I'm Detective Carolina McKay. The Pittsburgh City Police and FBI are investigating a missing woman. We tracked her phone and the man in possession of it, bought it here. Now I expect some cooperation or we'll have a dozen cops raiding this place in a hot minute."

The woman's nose crinkled and she pulled her head backward, turning two chins into four. "Jesus," she said. "Don't gotta be a bitch about it. I just work here. Owner's in the back. I'll get him."

"Thank you," Carolina said, wishing she didn't have to keep pushing people for information.

"Not bad," Max said when the woman was gone. "You didn't even have to assault her."

"Suppose I could have let you flirt with her. You're probably her type."

"What's that? Dashing? Handsome? Muscular?" Max asked.

Carolina rolled her eyes. "Sure. All of the above." She fake coughed. No sense letting his ego get any bigger.

Max looked past her. "Pretty sure I'm not this one's type. Better work your magic," he said.

Carolina followed his gaze and found a man who made Danny DeVito look tall and fit shuffling toward them. He wore glasses that turned his eyes into saucers and a green-gray growth the size of an acorn clung to his upper lip. Carolina couldn't help but stare.

"You people have a court order?" he asked.

Just like that, Carolina thought. No pleasantries or even idle curiosity about the matter at hand. No apology for selling stolen merchandise. Just straight in with the legalese. No wonder she hated people.

Carolina half-turned toward Max and slipped him Jack's business card without the pawn shop's owner noticing. Max stepped around her and held it up for the short man to inspect.

"I was hoping that wouldn't be necessary as time is of the essence," Max said. "But if you need me to call the DA and make that happen, just say the word. Of course, then we'll have to get thorough and go through your records." His smile returned. "But I'm sure everything is on the up and up and you wouldn't have anything to worry about. Right?"

The man gave a fast, nervous titter. The two of them played a game of chicken to see who would break first. Max didn't even blink.

"Alright, come back here," the owner said, beckoning them toward the offices with a thick hand. "I'm Mo Gladden," he said. "Owned this place forty-three years and I don't need you in here threatening my livelihood or the customers that come in. So spit it out."

They stepped into his office and he closed the door behind them. Then, Mo slid behind a desk and plopped into what looked like the kind of booster chair children use in restaurants. His fingers went to work on a keyboard which sat behind an old school CRT computer monitor.

"We need to know who you bought a phone from," Carolina said.

"A phone?" Mo burped up a laugh. "You have any idea how many fucking phones I sell a week? I'm gonna need a date, a name, something specific, otherwise you're just pissing in the wind."

"It was sold three days ago. Buyer was Siraji Amiri," Carolina said.

"You're gonna have to spell that," Mo said.

She did and he typed. Seconds later he swiveled the monitor so they could see it.

"That the one?" he asked.

Carolina nodded, eyes flitting across the screen. She saw that Mo had paid sixty dollars for it and sold it for two-hundred and fifty. "Hundred and ninety buck profit? Pretty sweet deal."

"If you can get it," Mo said. "This guy, Felix, comes by with a bunch of stuff. Usually I make an offer on the whole lot, that way I don't have to fish through all the shit. Most of the time it works out in my favor."

"Felix?"

"Yeah, he's a regular. In and out every couple a weeks."

"Does he have a last name?" Carolina asked.

Mo twitched his lip, causing the growth to shimmy like a Hawaiian belly dancer. Carolina's stomach churned at the sight. "Duchamp," Mo said.

"You got an address for Felix Duchamp?"

Mo shook his head like that was the dumbest question he was ever asked. "He's a customer. I don't go to his house for poker night and pool parties."

Max leaned in, towering over. "Sir, please understand the seriousness of this situation."

Carolina held back a smirk of her own. Max was good at this.

Mo sighed. "He runs a motel out by the airport.

Thunderbird Inn. Most of the crap he brings is shit guests leave behind. Never nothing stolen. I don't do that kind of business here."

"Isn't that what a lost and found is for?" Carolina asked.

Mo shrugged. "Hey, who am I to tell another guy how to run his business?"

Carolina spun toward the door, Max tagging along with her. She was on the verge of a clean, classy getaway but couldn't stop herself. "You open to some advice?"

"Depends on the advice," Mo said.

"Get that fucking tumor cut off your lip."

CHAPTER NINETEEN

"Yet another shithole," Carolina said, staring at the run-down, one-story motel.

Max stood with her outside the Prius. "Aren't you used to this by now?"

The Thunderbird Inn wasn't the kind of place she'd have stayed if it was the only motel on the planet. The plaster facade was coming off in chunks and the parking lot was more potholes than pavement. It looked abandoned, but a smattering of vehicles said otherwise.

How could Scarlet earn enough cash to live such a lavish lifestyle working in places like this? It made no sense.

"I suppose I expected something classier," she said to Max.

He laughed. "If I remember correctly, it wasn't very long ago that you and I were shacked up at a motel not worlds better than this one. And I don't recall you complaining."

She stared at him deadpan, clucking her tongue. "You really had to go there, didn't you?" she asked. "Get your jabs in about our forgettable little tryst. Clearly it made more of an impression on you than me."

As she headed to the lobby door, she glanced back at Max and found him slouching against the hood of the car. He wasn't smiling, he was pouting.

"Well?" she asked.

Max made a shooing motion. "Go ahead. I'm gonna sit this one out. Don't shoot anybody."

She was shocked her dig had done some damage. What happened to the kid's swagger? "Max, I didn—"

Overhead a 747 roared as it took off, the noise drowning out all other sound. It was just as well. She wasn't sure what to say.

As the thundering of the jet engines faded, Max turned from her. "It's fine, Carolina. Go ahead and pretend you're still a cop." He strode away from the car, past the rows of rooms, exploring.

His pity party act annoyed her, but she couldn't help feeling guilty. They'd worked so well together at the pawn shop, and he'd come all this way for her. She didn't want to fuck that up. Next time, she'd have to remember that Max was more delicate than her. Hell, that was true about most men.

She pulled the door open and stepped into a stuffy, small lobby that reeked of patchouli. There were no amenities, not even a coffee machine. There was also no clerk waiting behind the desk, just a TV on the wall showing professional bowling on ESPN.

There was no bell to ding for service either, so she used her voice. "Hey? Anybody home?" She banged the counter for effect, then regretted it as the counter was so sticky it could have been slathered in honey.

As she wiped her hand on her jeans, and yearned for sanitizer, she heard glass break in the room behind the office. "Hey?" she called out. The only response was more clattering.

"Oh, damn it."

She jumped over the counter, an act that caused screaming

pain in her broken ribs, and a few other places for laughs, pushed open the door to the office, and checked the room. The first thing she saw was a broken lamp on the floor. The second was a man in the process of climbing out the window.

He was tall and lanky and had his legs all the way through, holding the frame with his hands. He shot a glance toward Carolina as her pounding footsteps nabbed his attention.

"Stop!" Carolina shouted, but it was no use. The man dropped outside and was gone. "Motherfucker!"

She raced to the window and saw him running full tilt. "I'm not a cop, asshole!"

He didn't slow and she knew her only chance of catching up with him was following the same course. As much as her pained body begged her not to, she scrambled through the window, dropping hard to the pavement below, and chased.

The man collided with a tower of unfolded cardboard boxes, sending them tumbling sideways. Carolina had to hurdle them, but didn't slow.

She hated running, always had, and this was no exception. When the man rounded a corner, she managed to pick up her pace even further. Her ribs sang out in protest, then her shoulder joined the chorus. She was going to really hate herself when this was over.

Even at this rate, her odds of catching him were slim. She half-expected him to have vanished when she came around the corner but he was still there, gaining on her.

Ahead, stood a three feet high cinder block wall that separated the motel's parking lot from the neighboring Arby's. He was going for it, then suddenly zigged instead of zagged, slipping between the motel and a small storage shed.

I'm going to lose this prick, Carolina thought and tried to run even faster, but she was fading fast. He was out of her sight for a good ten seconds before she reached that gap and she knew he would be gone when she passed through it.

Instead, he was flat on his back, rocking side to side, and holding his face with both hands. Blood seeped between his fingers.

Max stood over him, holding a broken piece of hardwood from a shipping pallet.

"You broke my nose!" the man on the ground grumbled.

Carolina looked to Max, curious about what had just transpired.

He shrugged. "I saw the fool running blind, held the board up about face level. He ran into it." Max set the makeshift weapon aside, leaning it against the shed. Then he reached into his pocket, pulled out a handkerchief, and handed it to the man. "You should be more observant."

"Fuck you!" The man took it and held it to his nose. Blood quickly saturated the rag.

About that time, Carolina finally caught up. She planted her hands on her thighs, bending at the waist as she tried to catch her breath.

"Fancy seeing you here," Max said. There was no hint of hurt in his voice. In fact, it was smug and mocking.

"Really?" she asked, still panting. She pointed at the man on the ground. "This whole thing... What I said to you... None of it..." She couldn't finish her sentences and wasn't sure if she made any sense, but Max caught her drift.

"I heard something break, figured you might have yourself a runner," Max said.

"I don't hold grudges."

"Quick thinking. And thanks."

Max nodded. "For you? Anytime."

The man groaned, garnering their attention. He was in his late forties with a carrot-colored mop of hair that hung to his shoulders in out of control curls. "I need a doctor! I could have a deviated septum!"

Carolina moved to his side and crouched. She grabbed his

right wrist and jerked it away from his nose. It looked straight enough to her. "It's not even broken, you pussy."

"I heard a crack," he said, pushing himself into a sitting position. The bleeding had already slowed to a trickle. "I think I have a concussion. Maybe a skull fracture."

"If you're planning a lawsuit, you should know I'm unemployed and my friend here is an amateur journalist."

The man looked from Carolina to Max, then back. "Aw, fuck." He stood, tossing Max's handkerchief onto the ground.

"Felix Duchamp?" Carolina asked him.

"The fuck it is to you?"

Such a charmer. "Why'd you run?"

He seemed to consider the question. "Instinct. You're a cop, right?"

"I'm not," Carolina said, ignoring Max's resulting smirk.

"Well then I ain't saying shit."

Carolina stepped into his personal space. "You most definitely will be talking to me. Otherwise I'll call the cops and tell them about all the guest property you sell to Downtown Pawn."

Felix sneered revealing blood stained, horsey teeth. "Aw, stick your thumb up your twat. That's shit people leave behind when they check out. I got no responsibility to hold it."

He stomped away, purposely banging shoulders with her, hitting her bad shoulder. She gritted her teeth and tried not to let the pain show. The impact knocked a lone key on a ring loose from Felix's back pocket. She bent and grabbed it.

"Where's this open?" she asked.

"Give that back. That's hotel property," Felix demanded.

"Why'd you really run Felix?" she asked. "Does it have anything to do with my sister?"

"Lady, I don't know you from Eve, so I sure as shit don't know your sister."

Carolina pulled out a photo of Scarlet which she'd printed

at the apartment. She unfolded it and pushed it into the man's face. "You sold her iPhone to Mo Gladden less than a week ago. Hot pink case, rhinestones all over it. Ring any bells?"

"None. Now give me back my key." His eyes were past her though, staring at the corner room at the hotel upon which a handwritten sign hung. *Out of order.* People were such terrible liars.

"Come on," she said to Felix, then motioned for Max to bring up the rear. Max did, keeping his large hands squeezed tight against Felix's shoulders.

When they reached the room, Carolina slid the key into the lock and turned it. "Perfect fit." The lock snapped and she twisted the knob.

She glanced back at Max. "You got him?"

Max nodded, hands tightening on Felix's traps. "I got him."

Carolina pocketed the key, then gripped her pistol as she eased the door open. She didn't know what to expect, what she was going to find.

This man, who took off running at the first sign of trouble, had a secret room at the same motel where her sister's phone had supposedly been abandoned. She felt nervous and sick as she stepped through the doorway.

But instead of finding Scarlet—bound and held captive, or worse, dead—she found a vacant room bathed in blue, ultraviolet light. Carolina had seen enough grow houses during her time on the Baltimore PD to know immediately what she'd stepped into. And, as far as hydroponic, indoor marijuana growing stations, it wasn't half bad.

"Holy hell," Max said, peering over Carolina's shoulder.

Felix struggled, eager to flee again now that his operation had been exposed, but Max held firm.

"Come on, lady," Felix said. "You said you was here about your sister. As you can see, she ain't here."

Carolina turned back to the squirming man. "Fine," she

said. "But tell me where you got her phone. You do that and I won't call Sergeant Terrell Werner of the Pittsburgh City Police and tip him to your side business."

Felix shook his head. "I don't know, it's just a phone."

Carolina slapped him in the cheek hard enough to raise a welt.

"Fuck off!" Felix spat.

Carolina slapped him even harder. And then again and again until her hand tired out. Max didn't stop her, but she knew if she balled her fist, he would have put a stop to it.

"What's your fucking problem, man? If you didn't do anything to her, then why won't you answer a simple question?" She was so close to his face that she could smell the roast beef and cheese he had for lunch.

She pulled out her flip phone and opened it. "Tell me, shit head. You've got as long as it takes me to punch ten numbers on the keypad." She began to dial.

Self-preservation kicked in for Felix. "I just found it in a room. Left on top of the dresser. But I don't know shit about your sister lady."

"Was anything else left behind?"

"No. I swear."

After taking a long look at him, she pushed past Max and Felix, heading toward the exit. "Let him go," Carolina told Max and he did.

Felix closed and locked the door to the motel room. When they were halfway to the Prius, he shouted to them. "So we're cool, right? You aren't gonna narc on me?"

Carolina opened the passenger side door and looked back to him. "I haven't decided yet. So, it's up to you whether you want to leave that op in the room and hope I'm a nice person or dispose of it all on the chance I feel like being a bitch. Enjoy the rest of your life, dick face."

CHAPTER TWENTY

Max threw down the bag of takeout on the kitchen island. After the run-in with Felix Duchamp she had a hankering for Primanti's and the two of them brought back a good haul. She'd tried to explain to Max the appeal of a sandwich loaded down with French fries and coleslaw, but he wasn't buying it.

"Just wait," she said. "You'll like it."

And he did. Both were so famished they wolfed down half their meal before even discussing the day's events. By the time they stopped for a breath, Max had coleslaw dressing dribbling from both corners of his mouth. The sight made Carolina happy for the first time all day.

"I told you," Carolina said, her own mouth half full.

Max nodded, too busy eating to respond verbally.

Her thoughts quickly shifted back to the task at hand, though. Where did they go from here?

Scarlet running off and leaving her phone behind made no sense. What did make sense, what she didn't want to consider, was that something bad had happened in that motel room. Had her sister survived it?

"Forgive me if this is a dumb question," Carolina said. "But you said iPhones and iPads synced. Does that mean copies of the same data is on both?"

"Some parts. Not like documents and apps, but photos and emails, yeah."

"What about address books?"

"Like phone contacts? Because I don't think anyone under the age of fifty actually keeps an address book anymore." He took another bite of food.

"The phone contacts on the iPad were empty," Carolina said, annoyed that her lone idea was shot down so quickly.

Max shook his head. "Her contacts were, yeah. But we didn't check her FaceTime."

"Can you do that?"

He grinned as he wiped his mouth clean with the back of his hand. "Yeah, I think I can manage." He grabbed the tablet from her, tapped away at the screen. "I have the last thirty days pulled up. Nothing for the last nine though. But there are a few numbers."

He turned the screen so she could see it. There were eight numbers listed, all women's names. "You recognize any of these?" he asked.

Carolina scanned the list. "Only my mother," she said. Who knew Beatrice Boothe could FaceTime?

The other names meant nothing. Erica. Gwen. Judy. Geena J. Geena T. Daria. Monica.

"They could be friends," Max suggested.

"Or clients," she said, again knowing very little about her sister's preferences.

"Nice," Max said, though immediately showing regret on his face. "Sorry."

She ignored him, grabbing her own phone and starting with

the first number on the list. It went to a voicemail. She decided not to leave a message, wanting to keep the upper hand in any subsequent conversations. She had no idea who these women were or if she could trust them.

After being met with more voicemail requests, the fifth number she tried picked up. The name was Geena J.

"Hello?" the woman on the other line asked.

"Geena?" Carolina asked.

"Who's asking?"

"My name is Carolina. I think you know my sister, Scarlet."

Geena went silent. If not for her breathing into the receiver Carolina would have thought the call was cut off.

"Geena? Please."

Finally, she responded. "I didn't know Scarlet had a sister."

"Most don't. And she does. A half-sister anyway."

"Look, I don't know why you're calling me or how you got this number but—"

"I'm sorry. Just give me a minute to explain, okay?"

Silence. She took that as an affirmative.

"No one's been able to get in touch with Scarlet for over a week. She hasn't shown up for work. And our mother's ready to stroke out with worry. I know nothing about my sister's friends, but found your number on her iPad. I really need some help here." She waited, hopeful that was enough.

"Fuck," Geena said under her breath, though if Carolina wasn't listening intently, she would have missed it.

"Do you know where she is?" Carolina asked.

"I don't want to talk on the phone. Can you meet me?" Geena asked.

Carolina didn't like it, having no idea who this person was or if she was involved with her sister's disappearance, but she had few other options. "Yes, but—"

"In a public place," Geena said.

"You read my mind," Carolina answered.

"Good. Now, don't take offense to this, but come alone. If I see anyone I even think is with you, I turn into a ghost."

"Understandable," Carolina said.

"Good. I'll text you the address. When you get there, ask for Meryl." Geena ended the call before Carolina could say anything more.

Her phone dinged and a text came through with the address.

"Looks like I'm flying solo on this one," she told Max.

CHAPTER TWENTY-ONE

She was grateful Max let her borrow the Prius, but even that car was out of place at the restaurant connected to the address Geena J had sent. The cars in the lot were shiny and expensive. Range Rovers, G Wagons, even a Bentley. Toys belonging to people with bigger wallets than souls.

Max had stayed behind at the apartment, promising to mine the iPad for any other information or contacts they might have missed. Though she made sure to give him the evilest of evil eyes as she warned him not to peruse the risqué photos of her sister. He'd feigned offense and crossed his heart, then gave her a scout's honor promise and held up some random fingers.

If she were a betting woman, she would have put money down that he didn't even know what Webelos stood for.

She drove to the valet station, met by a man in a red vest. As she exited the car and handed over the keys, he waited with a prissy smile on his round face.

Fuck, was she expected to tip on the way in and the way out? She greased his palm with a five dollar bill. When he saw what it was, his prissy smile turned to disgust.

"You're lucky you got that much," she said. "Now don't scratch the paint. It's a rental."

She smirked as she strutted away. She wasn't a rich bitch, but she enjoyed pretending.

Another employee held the door for her as she stepped into the restaurant. The lighting was dim and dramatic. Ambiance, probably, for wealthy people, but she was more concerned about walking into a table or knocking over a chair.

Carolina hadn't made it ten feet inside when the maître d' stepped around the corner. He wore a perfectly fitting tuxedo while she'd shown up in jeans, an old cardigan, and her Chuck Taylors.

"Welcome to Savuer Riviere," he said and she swore he put on a fake French accent when he said it. Before she could respond he gave her the once over, not bothering to mask his disapproval. "Unfortunately we are reservation only. If you would like to call ahead at a later date we would be happy to—"

"I'm meeting a friend," Carolina said. "Meryl."

The man paused, skeptical. "I see." He reviewed a leather booklet, checking names. "One moment, please." He disappeared behind the wall separating the lobby from the dining area.

She took a few steps forward, trying to see where he went, but was wary of being too obvious. All she needed was to get thrown out of this snooty joint.

A few moments later, he returned. "Follow me, please."

She followed, passing between tables, and was led to a seating area with a view of the city. A woman sat alone, sipping on a glass of wine. She had legs that would have reached Carolina's chest and perfectly coiffed jet black hair. She was somewhere in her late twenties and wore a dress that looked like she belonged in a place such as this. Unlike Carolina.

"If there's anything else you need, please ask. We are at your service," the host said and walked off.

Carolina took the chair opposite Geena. She looked outside and saw the river below, not realizing how underwhelming the view would be. The sky was gunmetal gray and featureless, the water was murky and lazy. Rather than sailboats and yachts, it held ships carrying freight and tug boats. The view from here made Pittsburgh look industrial and depressing and was hardly worthy of fine dining ambiance.

"You're Scarlet's sister?" Geena asked, disbelief coming through in just three short words.

Carolina turned to her, taking a long look. Despite how beautiful the woman was, it all seemed manufactured. Her breasts were huge, but too high on her chest and looked hard as petrified wood. Her lips might have been perfect for blow jobs, but almost comically oversized. There wasn't a wrinkle or smile line to be seen on her face. She might still be young, but already worshipped at the Botox altar.

"I am," Carolina said.

Geena evaluated Carolina the same way and seemed equally unimpressed. "You don't look like her."

"So I've been told," Carolina said.

A waiter sidled up beside the table. He was graying and in his fifties and dapper in his suit. Carolina thought him quite handsome, but all his attention was on Geena and he had no shame in staring down her dress as he spoke. "Good afternoon, ladies. My name is Samuel. May I take your order?"

"I'll have the Summer Tomato Bouillabaisse with Basil Rouille," Geena said.

The waiter smiled, his cheeks glowing red. "That is a wonderful, wonderful choice."

Carolina watched as the waiter had to pry his eyes from Geena to take her order, but she hadn't even looked at the menu. It mattered not as she was still full of the sandwiches she'd shared with Max. "Can I just have a cup of soup?"

Samuel the waiter's eyes narrowed. "A cup of soup?"

Carolina nodded. "Beef barley, if you have it."

He coughed a dismissive laugh. "I'm afraid we do not. The choices are oille, potée, ragout fin, and bouillabaisse."

She had no idea what any of those were and only recognized the latter because Geena had just ordered it. "The last one."

Samuel nodded. "And to drink? We have a lovely assortment of aged wines from the—"

"Diet Coke."

The waiter visibly held in his derision, then turned and left them.

After that humiliation, it was time to get back to business. "You and Scarlet are friends?"

Geena took a long drink of her wine. "One could say that."

"And how would you say it?" she asked.

"We worked together. But yes, a friendship has been building."

Carolina was certain this woman didn't work at the Golden Waters Casino. "Worked together? Are you a client of hers?"

Geena eyed Carolina, a sort of bemused skepticism on her perfect, stony face. "I'm unsure how educated you are as to your sister's profession."

Snooty bitch, Carolina thought. Time to bring her down a peg. "I know that she exchanges sexual favors for money and apparently does quite well at it. Am I missing anything?"

Geena gave a humorless smile. "Yes, you are most certainly missing something." Another swallow of wine finished the glass. Carolina thought, if she got drunk, maybe she'd be nicer.

"It's much more than the physical acts. We provide emotional support for our clients and genuine affection. We listen to them, care about them. We give them a full experience. It may culminate in the bedroom, but it's not some seedy, base act as you're inferring."

Carolina thought of an old saying about putting lipstick on

a pig, but refrained from sharing that with Geena. "I get it. I'm not judging you or Scarlet and I'm sorry if it came off that way."

"It did. And I accept your apology."

To Carolina's surprise, the brief tiff seemed to relax the woman. The tension went out of her shoulders and she almost looked human rather than sexbot.

"Scarlet and I are paid companions. We're not prostitutes that you pick up on street corners. We are paid to be beautiful, to be cultured, and perhaps most of all, discreet. It's about the image, the experience, that we afford. If all our gentlemen wanted was sex, they wouldn't need, and most certainly could not afford, women of our caliber."

Carolina listened, patient. She didn't like what she was hearing, but Geena's spin made her feel somewhat better. If anything, she had to admit, Geena was a good salesperson.

"Alright, so you're not a client, but you worked with her. In, like..." She searched for a better word but couldn't come up with one. "Threesomes?"

That actually made Geena laugh, albeit in a very reserved manner.

"At parties. Oftentimes clients will fly multiple girls to their vacation homes or to special events. Nothing makes a man feel more masculine than being surrounded by beautiful women for all the world to see. But that's where the working together ended," she said.

She leaned in over the table, giving Carolina an even better view of her ample breasts as they pushed up in her dress. "You may look down on our profession, but fitting into that lifestyle seamlessly is a skill to itself. We have girls with master's degrees and PHDs. The gentlemen want someone who can keep up with them on an intellectual level as much as physical."

Carolina was shocked. And then she realized that maybe she was being too judgmental. It wasn't a lifestyle she'd ever care to try out, but here was Geena being treated with respect at a Michelin star restaurant while she was looked at like something undesirable stuck on your shoe.

"How long have you known Scarlet?" Carolina asked.

"Two, maybe three years. There aren't many here, only a few dozen, so we tend to stick together."

"Why are you in Pittsburgh? I mean, compared to New York City or Los Angeles or Miami? Isn't this place a little..." She looked again to the drab view.

"Depressing?"

Carolina nodded.

"With the airport nearby we can be anywhere we want to be. We get put on international flights, domestic flights. And the cost of living is fantastic. More bang for our buck living here. No pun intended," Geena said with a wink.

Carolina thought for sure that pun was intended.

"Do you think Scarlet is on one of these excursions now? Maybe flown out to Vegas or something?"

The boozy cheer faded from Geena. "Possibly, but it's unlikely. Our little group tends to keep each other in the loop when it comes to travel, and she never told me she was leaving town."

That had been one of Carolina's last hopes and having it dashed hurt. "How scared should I be?" she asked.

Geena paused, long enough for it to become worrisome. "Under normal circumstances, I'd say not very. This business is transient and there's always the possibility that she had to relocate and didn't want anyone knowing her whereabouts. Once in a while a client gets too... attached, and such actions become a necessity."

"Like stalkers?"

Geena nodded.

"Did Scarlet ever mention anyone like that?"

"Not to me."

"So what do you mean, *under normal circumstances?*

What's abnormal about this?"

It was Geena's turn to take in the bland cityscape. She was still looking at it when she got around to answering. "Two other girls have checked out over the last few weeks."

"Checked out? You mean disappeared?"

Another nod. "Possibly."

"Have you gone to the police about this?"

Geena huffed. "Of course not."

"Would you? I have a contact there. I can go with you to make a statement."

The woman turned to her, eyes cold and hard. "No, I would not. Do you think I want to get arrested? To have everything I've worked for stolen from me? For all I know the girls fell in love, ran off, and got married. It happens more than you'd think and when it does, they don't exactly keep in contact with old colleagues."

"Pretty Woman," Carolina added.

"Except she was a streetwalker. That cow didn't know class if it slapped her in the face."

"But Scarlet wouldn't cut off our mother. They're close. If you'd just talk to the police with me, maybe we can—"

Geena jumped up, sending her chair clattering backward. It threatened to tip but steadied at the last moment. "I told you what I know. More than I should have. And I don't appreciate this harassment."

She turned to leave but Carolina lunged out, caught her wrist. "If you were ever her friend, you owe this to her."

Geena yanked her arm free. "At least I knew your sister. It's obvious you never did."

Carolina was going to say something clever, but when it came down to it, Geena was right. The woman stomped away, brushing past Samuel who was just then returning with their food.

Damn it, now she was stuck with the bill.

CHAPTER TWENTY-TWO

Even though his shift was over, Terrell Werner agreed to meet Carolina at Ralph's Coffee. After filling up a thermos with the brew, he returned to the wobbly table where she sat and eased himself into a chair across from her, extra careful in case it might break. It was stronger than it looked.

"You said on the phone you have information on your sister," he said.

Carolina nodded. "You heard about what really happened at the casino, right?"

He broke into a wide grin. "Oh yeah, I heard. Randy Drake's quite the celebrity, for all the wrong reasons."

"So it's clear Scarlet wasn't involved. But she's still missing. And I might have some leads."

Terrell took a drink from the thermos, then set it on the table. "Sure you don't want any? Or something to eat?"

The last thing she wanted was more food. After Geena J abandoned her at the snooty French restaurant she wasn't about to throw away the sixty-four dollars the food had cost and consumed all of it herself, leaving her feeling ready to burst. "No, I'm good."

"If you say so." He chomped a bite from a danish. "Don't know what you're missing though."

"Back to Scarlet," Carolina said, trying to steer the conversation somewhere productive.

"Oh, yeah. What'd you find out?"

"Well, to start, she didn't just work at the casino. Her real job, at least, the one where she made the most money, was as an escort."

He let loose a low whistle then shook his head in judgment.

"Ultra high end though. The type that gets flown to tropical places, invited to parties with the rich and richer. High-end clientele, to say the least."

"I see."

"I tracked her cell phone and found out it had been pawned downtown. From there I backtraced it to a hotel by the airport. That's where things dead end, at least so far."

"The Hyatt?" Terrell asked, finishing the Danish a second bite.

"No. A place called the Thunderbird Inn."

His eyes narrowed but he didn't speak again until he chewed and swallowed the pastry. "Thunderbird's a dive. I wouldn't board my dog there."

She thought about telling him of Felix's amateur grow op but didn't want the sergeant to get distracted. "There's no evidence she was actually there. Just her phone. My theory is that the person responsible for her disappearance was staying there."

Terrell humored that notion. "Or maybe she was there seeing a john. They rent rooms by the hour, you know."

Carolina chewed the inside of her cheek, trying to keep her temper in check. "She's not that kind of escort."

The man raised a curious eyebrow. "This sister of yours.

She have any substance abuse problems? Meth's what we see most often these days. But crack's still around. Heroin too."

"Why would you even ask that?"

He pursed his lips in annoyance. "Carolina, I know she's your sister, but you have to go into this with your eyes wide open. Women don't become involved in that lifestyle out of choice. They do it out of necessity. To feed a bad habit."

"I don't mean any offense by this, but you're the one with your eyes closed, Sergeant. I'm telling you information I've dug up about my sister while your department has done all of jack and shit and you're sitting here lecturing me about her potential drug habits. That's fucked up."

Yeah, he would probably be offended by that.

Terrell leaned back in his chair, which gave a small scream of duress. "You know how many missing persons reports we get on girls like your sister every year? And nine times out of ten they show up a week or two later strung out in an alley or in the E.R. Overdosed on whatever shit they've been shooting up their arms or sniffing up their noses."

"What about the other one? The tenth woman who doesn't turn up at all?"

He didn't have a quick comeback for that and bought time by wiping crumbs from his tie.

"Scarlet isn't the only one, either. I spoke with a colleague of hers. Two other women have gone missing recently. How many more will it be before you take this seriously?"

"I'll put a note in the file, but people aren't going to get their panties in a bunch over a bunch of missing hookers. I hate to say it, but it's a dangerous job they chose, not to mention illegal, and they know the risks."

Carolina slammed her hand on the table and jumped to her feet. "This is unbelievable. If you won't do your fucking job, then I will."

Terrell sipped his coffee. "Have at it. Pay isn't that great but city benefits are top notch." Then he had the audacity to laugh.

She could still hear that booming, baritone guffaw when she hit the sidewalk. Carolina wasn't sure why she was so shocked, she knew cops' opinions on sex workers. But she was. Maybe because Elven had vouched for him. Or maybe because she'd made the mistake of thinking there were still men who cared about saving women's lives, regardless of their professions or demons. As usual, she'd expected too much and it was time to get back to being a cynic and taking matters into her own hands.

CHAPTER TWENTY-THREE

SCARLET'S CAPTOR HADN'T BEEN AROUND TO TORMENT her at all that day and she used the reprieve to work at her restraints. The metal cuff on her ankle had cut her almost to the bone. Every time she tried to force it further down on her foot it dug deeper, slicing into muscles and tendons.

Her broken left hand further hampered her efforts. She was close to losing hope, to giving up. Part of her already had, but there was a sliver of strength, of fortitude, deep inside that told her she still had a chance.

But that part grew smaller with each passing hour.

Earlier in the day she gave up on the cuff, it was too painful, and moved to the wall where the chain was bolted down, rocking it back and forth. Back and forth. Back and forth. The wood seemed to be weakening, softening.

"Come on," she said, shocking herself with the sound of her hoarse, raspy voice. "Give me a fucking break already."

She took a deep breath, steeling herself, gathering her strength. Then, she pulled with all her remaining effort, using her body weight, using everything she had, throwing herself backward.

The chain held.

But did she hear a crack? She scrambled toward the bolts, trying to see in the near dark. Was the wood splintering or was it her imagination playing tricks? Like a mirage in a desert.

Scarlet steeled herself for another try when—

A shrill scream pierced the night air.

She froze, listening.

Tires gritted in the gravel. Her heart sank.

He was back.

A vehicle door opened. Closed.

"No!" a woman screamed. "Let me go!"

He had a new girl. A new victim.

Did that mean that she was the new Eve? Did that mean that her days were counting down faster now? Scarlet scrambled to the sliver in the slats of the barn to get a good look.

He carried her over his shoulder. Her legs were wrapped in tape, but she flailed with her arms, battering his back.

"Oh honey, save your energy," Scarlet whispered.

As he stomped past the hogs, they snorted. Eager, hungry. Ready for a fresh meal.

It'll be me, in their bellies. The thought didn't scare her as much as she feared it would. In fact, it brought a sort of relief. Maybe it would be better. If nothing else, it would be over.

There came a thud, a yelp. Then the barn door slid open.

Scarlet hurried to the front of the stall and saw the monster silhouetted by the moonlight. The girl was on the ground, squirming like an oversized worm. Before she could make any attempt at an escape, the man grabbed her by the feet and dragged her backward into the barn.

"Help!" the woman screamed. "Someone help me!"

Scarlet had tried screaming. She knew it was a waste of breath. Wherever they were was far away from listening ears.

The duo reached the stall where Eve had been chained. The man shoved the girl into it, then stomped on her midsection, knocking the air from her, turning her silent.

"Stay," he said in his deep and slow voice.

Scarlet didn't recognize her, but she fit the type. Buxom, beautiful. She wore a dress slitted nearly to her waist. Her overly dramatic makeup was tear-streaked and smeared. Straw had collected in her long, blonde hair.

This new girl didn't take orders. Instead, she kicked and screamed and tried to climb to her feet. She managed to stand, but with her legs tied all she could do was scoot her feet a few millimeters at a time. The man stepped in front of her, blocking her path.

She screamed in response, right in his face.

This made him angry. He grabbed her by the hair and snapped her head back. Then he leaned over her, pressing his feral face tight against his newest captive's, and he screamed back.

Then he shoved her and she tripped over her feet, falling, colliding with the stable wall. Cracking her head on the way down.

She didn't get back up.

"Good," he said, crouching down and grabbing the chain which had once held Eve. He put the cuff around this new girl's leg, then took a key from his pocket and locked it in place. He gave it a hard yank to ensure it was fastened. It was.

With that finished, he unbound the girl's legs. No need for tape now. She wasn't going anywhere.

He stood, one hand scratching at his crotch, the other pushing his hair out of his face so he could get a good look at his newest toy. Then he began to unbutton his jeans. They dropped to the floor in a heap, exposing his shit-smeared ass.

Scarlet knew this might be her last chance. She stood, slow. Careful not to make a sound. Her eyes were glued on the half-dressed man as he crouched in front of the girl, shoving her legs apart.

She was woozy from her fall, conscious but incapable of resisting. The man reached to her groin, grabbed her panties in his fist and ripped them away.

Scarlet moved to the wall, trying to remember her lone season of track and field back in Dupray, West Virginia. She crouched in a sprinter's stance.

The man thrust himself into the semi-conscious woman. Scarlet felt her heart break for the girl, but she needed this distraction.

She knew this was going to hurt, that it might seal her fate, but it was all she had. Scarlet exploded out of her crouch, running full tilt. It was only two yards before the chain reached its limit, but when it did—

The wood snapped. The bolts tore loose from the wall.

She was free.

The man was so caught up in the rape, in the savage attack, he never heard the commotion. She knew she should attack him. She should grab some tool and bash his skull in. She should save not only herself, but this new victim.

Those were all things she should have done. What a good person would have done. But Scarlet cared more about surviving than being a good person.

So she ran.

CHAPTER TWENTY-FOUR

After meeting with Terrell Werner, Carolina was livid. She explained what went down to Max, and telling him they were on their own. After he talked her down the two tried to hatch a new plan, but despite hours of brainstorming they were stuck.

Max offered to take her out, to get her mind off things but that was the opposite of what Carolina wanted. She needed to find a crack, a hole, something she could exploit. As she tossed and turned in bed, she kept coming up empty.

She knew she should text Bea and tell her what was happening—or not happening. Part of her even wanted to ask their mother if she was aware of Scarlet's secret life. Maybe she knew some of Scarlet's contacts in that world. After all, what else would the two of them talk about twice weekly?

But she wasn't up for her mother tonight. She wasn't up for anything but escape.

Carolina grabbed the stolen bottle of Percocet, now two thirds empty, and shook three into her palm. Just before she could take them, she put one back. She still hadn't talked to any of her doctors and secured her own supply so she needed to ration them.

After dropping the two pills on her tongue, she ground them between her teeth, relishing the sweet release that came seconds later.

It all faded. Her weeks in Monacan, Der Todesbringer, all the dead girls. Lester. Her pain went away too, like someone was slowly turning the faucet that allowed misery to flow through her body unabated.

The stress, the anxiety, the depression, the fear, all her emotions dulled to the point where they no longer existed and she eagerly floated into the fog of nothingness.

CHAPTER TWENTY-FIVE

She pumped her legs as fast as they would go. It had been over a week since she'd been able to fully utilize them and now her muscles cramped and burned, but she powered through. She had to. As much as she wanted to stop, rest, massage her legs, she knew there was no time. Not if she wanted to live.

This was her first look at a world outside the barn. She spotted a farmhouse. Fencing. And a lot of nothingness.

She saw a dirt road in the distance, but knew that would be the first place he'd look for her. To the east laid a dense forest. It offered the cover she needed.

Scarlet was less than twenty yards into the trees when she heard the man scream. She knew he would soon be on her trail and quickened her pace.

Minutes passed in what felt like hours. Leafless branches clawed at her face, scratched at her torso. The chain dragged behind her, getting caught on random brush, further aggravating the wound on her leg. She paused for only a second, gathering together the chain, carrying it. Then she was running again.

The rugged forest floor shredded her bare feet. She felt her big toenail catch on a rock, arc upward, and rip free in a searing flare of misery. She screamed, helpless to stop herself.

"I'll get you!" the man called in the distance. He didn't sound close but it was hard to be certain. She couldn't stop, couldn't commiserate with her pain. She had to keep running.

She imagined that he was just one tree away from her. It kept her going. She didn't risk a glance back. Anything that drew her attention away from going forward would get her caught.

And then she heard a new noise. Something different from the crickets and owls. Something unnatural.

Traffic.

A hillside loomed ahead. She was sure the sound emanated beyond it, so she scrambled up, hands clawing, feet digging at the loose soil.

"Girly..." the man called out. Closer.

She wouldn't look. She kept climbing.

Footfalls. Even closer.

She crested the hill. Below and beyond laid a narrow, two-lane road. It was her salvation. She could sense it.

Scarlet ran down the embankment, quickly losing her footing, falling. She tumbled, somersaulting, ricocheting off trees. She was the ball in a pinball machine careening out of control.

"Hey girly."

After falling for what felt like forever, her wanton motion stopped. She was in a ditch, frigid water soaking the scraps of clothing that still remained on her body.

She bounced to her feet, finding strength she never knew she had, pushing through the pain that fired in every nerve in her body, and ran for the road.

But before she made it into the clearing, he caught her, jerking her backward.

She knew it was him. He had grabbed her blouse and had her. Would drag her back to the barn where he'd rape her some more, then kill her, and feed her to the hogs.

She screamed and swatted at him, swinging the chain, weaponizing it.

But he wasn't there.

Her shirt was caught on a scraggly dead tree limb that hung low. She almost laughed, but she heard his footsteps in the underbrush, closer than ever. Ripping the material off the branch, she ran for the road.

"I got you now," he called.

That time it was so close she couldn't stop herself from looking. And she saw him. He was only a few long strides away.

His ratty, horrid face was washed in glee. He was enjoying this. It was all a game to him. A life and death version of hide and seek.

And he was about to win.

Not if I can do anything about it, she thought.

She spun back to the road, running again. The cool asphalt felt like clouds underfoot in comparison to the ragged turf of the woods. She sprinted with renewed energy and hope.

Let someone come along, she thought. A guy on his way home from the bar. A kid finishing up night shift at McDonald's. Somebody. Anybody. She only needed one car, one good Samaritan.

But there was no one. The road was vacant, not a headlight or taillight in sight.

This didn't make sense. She'd heard traffic from the woods. She still heard it. But where was it?

More running. More chasing. She was tiring. Wearing out. She couldn't keep this up much longer.

Behind her, the monster laughed. A huffing *heh hehe heh*

sound. The realization that he was going to catch her, that she was going to be subjected to his perverse torture again. The truth of that made tears spring from her eyes. They glistened in the moonlight as her run slowed to a jog.

Then she saw the road ahead change, narrowing into an overpass. And the sound of traffic grew louder.

This might be a rural road but below that was a highway. Freedom.

She planned to hurry down another hillside, toward that lower road, but a six-foot-tall fence, probably to deter deer from stumbling onto the four lane, blocked her path. Scarlet grabbed the wire, trying to climb it, but her broken hand was useless. Her shredded feet could find no hold. She fell off.

"Got ya now," the man said.

His progress had slowed too, but not out of exhaustion. He was taking his time to extend the game.

Her hands dug into the shale as she scrambled to her feet, then ran onto the bridge. The highway was fifteen feet below. Too far to jump and survive, she thought. But, if it came to it, that was a better outcome than rejoining this monster's own personal zoo from hell.

On the highway below, a tractor trailer approached, barreling along at seventy miles an hour. She waved her arms, trying to catch the driver's attention, but it was helpless. Hopeless.

The monster was closer. A good lunge and he'd have her. That wasn't going to happen though.

Scarlet climbed onto the concrete barrier that lined the overpass. Perched on it like a bird.

It was time to fly.

He dove for her, so close she felt the breeze of his arms arcing past her, just missing her.

She dropped through the air, only a second to pray she'd timed it right, then she hit.

Her body slammed into the top of the trailer with crushing ferocity. She bounced, floated, then landed again.

The wind whipped across her and, in the rapidly growing distance, she heard the monster scream, a sound akin to a wild dog howling at the moon.

Scarlet managed a weak yet triumphant smile, then everything went dark.

CHAPTER TWENTY-SIX

"Carolina." All was dark and she was moving, her body rocking.

The voice was loud and firm, but concerned too. Familiar.

"Carolina!"

It was Max's voice.

Her eyes didn't want to open, but she forced them. The man leaned over her, his arms on her shoulders, shaking her and not being gentle about it. His face was a mask of worry.

"Jesus," she said. "You sure know how to ruin a good night's sleep."

She was still hungover from the drugs, but the effect was fading quicker than she preferred. Already the pain in her ribs, her shoulder, had made itself known.

"I've been trying to wake you for fifteen minutes. I was about ready to call nine one one."

"You worry too much." Carolina sat up in the bed. Her mouth was still bitter from the taste of the Percocets and she reached for her mug on the nightstand. Only then did she notice the orange bottle still sitting there, in the open.

Her gaze went to Max and when he immediately broke eye contact she was certain he'd seen it. And that he knew.

"Or maybe I don't worry enough," he said, standing and taking a step away. She thought he was angry, but he was grabbing something. Her phone. He pushed it her way. "Your phone's been blowing up for the last half hour. It's your mom."

As soon as she accepted it, the phone buzzed as if backing up his story.

"Oh, shit." She flipped open the phone.

"Hey, Mom, sorry I haven't called, I've been—"

"They found Scarlet," Bea said, her voice high and anxious.

The tone of it made Carolina nervous because Bea didn't sound happy or relieved. She sounded scared.

She jolted upright in bed. The opioid fog lifting. "What do you mean by *found* her?"

Her heart raced and she was certain this was the baddest of bad news. Images of her sister's cold, lifeless body floated through her mind. Mutilation and gore. Blue tinted lips. All because she hadn't been able to piece together the puzzle fast enough.

"She's alive, Carolina. Thank, God!" Bea said, quashing the horror show Carolina had just created.

"Where is she? Who found her?"

Carolina was already out of bed. She stripped off the oversized t-shirt she'd slept in, not caring that it was all she was wearing. Max, who'd been watching this all unfold gawked wide-eyed for a moment, then spun away. His modesty shocked her.

As Carolina grabbed underwear and a bra off the floor, her mother kept speaking.

"She's been admitted to Old Miner's Hospital. I googled that." The thought of her mother googling something made Carolina smile. Or maybe it was just the relief of knowing her sister wasn't somewhere dead and hanging on a meat hook. "It's in Carrolltown, Pennsylvania."

"How is she?" Carolina had the panties on and was working at the bra, pinching the phone between her ear and shoulder.

"I didn't speak to her myself, not yet. Scarlet had one of the nurses call me. But she's coherent and stable. Can you go to her? I would but I don't trust myself driving that far in the state I'm in." Her voice was fragile and Carolina thought that wise.

"Yes. I'll leave now."

"Good."

The call ended. No thanks or I love you's. Some things never changed and, in a way, that familiarity was a relief.

Carolina tossed the phone onto the bed and grabbed a pair of jeans, looking to Max. "Look up the address for Old Miner's Hospital in Carrolltown, PA. Scarlet's there and we need to book it."

He risked a quick glance over his shoulder, saw she was no longer nude, and turned around. "Sorry for staring but I—"

"It's nothing you haven't seen before," she said, moving on to a sweater.

"True," Max said. "But I was pretty drunk then."

"As I recall, we both were."

He smiled. "Yeah. Don't get me wrong though, I enjoyed it. Then, and now."

Carolina managed a laugh, one that came easy and natural. It had been months, maybe longer, since she felt this unburdened. She could get used to this and hoped it lasted.

CHAPTER TWENTY-SEVEN

"More to the right," Scarlet said to the CNA who was adjusting the wall-mounted TV in her room.

"Now?" the CNA, a guy who didn't look old enough to have graduated high school, asked.

"A little more."

He turned it another fraction of an inch.

"Perfect," Scarlet said. "That takes care of the glare. Thank you, dear." She smiled a smile that was damn close to perfection despite everything she'd been through and the young man looked ready to dissolve into a puddle.

"Oh, any time, Miss Engle. If you need anything, just ask for me."

Carolina watched this exchange not with surprise, but a bit of awe. It was no wonder her sister was so good at her job. Not the casino gig, her real job.

When she had arrived at the hospital she'd done the usual *where's my sister* routine with the front desk. The place was aged and behind the times physically and that seemed to carry over into their privacy practices. There were no HIPPA hoops to jump through. Instead, an orderly took her straight to Scarlet's room on the third floor.

The GPS had said the drive would take the better part of two hours but the Prius was surprisingly swift and traffic was light early in the day. She and Max made it in under ninety minutes.

Upon hitting Scarlet's room, Carolina found the CNA attending to her needs and hovered unseen in the doorway. Max peeked past her, raising an eyebrow.

"What?" Carolina asked him.

Max leaned in close, his lips near enough to her ear to raise the temperature five degrees. "She doesn't hold a candle to you."

Despite herself, Carolina felt goosebumps break out on her forearms.

"I hate to sideline you, especially after that comment, but would you mind waiting in the lobby? My relationship with my sister is..."

He nodded. "I got you. It's cool."

She watched him leave and about that time the CNA was at the doorway. He seemed disappointed his private time with Scarlet Engle had been interrupted. "Are you family?" he asked.

Carolina looked past him, to her sister lying in the hospital bed. "About half," she said to the CNA who narrowed his eyes, then left the room.

At the sound of her voice, Scarlet pulled her attention away from the news, which was tuned in to the local broadcast, and looked at her with an expression between shock and distrust.

"Knock, knock," Carolina said from the doorway.

Scarlet sat up straighter in bed, wincing. "How did you—"

"Bea called me. Can I come in?"

"Of course."

Carolina stepped into the room, her nose assaulted by the

pungent antiseptic odor. There was a lone metal chair beside the bed and she put it to use. "How are you?"

"Alive," Scarlet said with a less perfect smile. "That's more than I thought I'd be twelve hours ago."

"I can see that much. I mean, how *are* you."

Whatever carefree facade her sister had built crumbled. Her lip quivered, pulling into a sneer and her tear ducts erupted. Carolina was never good with the touchy feely stuff and fumbled for a box of tissues on the stand beside the bed. Her hand was shaking though and she couldn't pull one free so she passed the whole box over. As she did, she realized Scarlet's left hand was in a cast, each of her fingers splinted. She wondered what other injuries the woman had suffered.

They were both silent for a long moment. Scarlet bundling up her emotions. Carolina at a loss for the right words. For maybe the first time in her life, she wished her mother was there.

"You drove all the way from Baltimore to see me?" Scarlet eventually got around to asking.

The question was a reminder of the chasm between them. Scarlet didn't even know that she'd left the city, temporarily moving home. Apparently her name never came up in those so frequent conversations with their mother. They shared half the same blood, but were strangers.

"Not exactly," Carolina said. "I've been in Pittsburgh. Looking for you."

"You?" Scarlet's voice broke.

Carolina nodded, but her mind was repeating *Don't cry again, Don't cry again*, on a loop inside her head. And a spiteful part she hated to acknowledge remembered her own time in the hospital, when Scarlet never even bothered to text to see how she was. But she didn't want to go there.

"Bea was worried because she hadn't heard from you. I

don't exactly have the busiest of lives these days, so she asked me to come up here and dig around."

Scarlet didn't cry, but she did something even more surprising. She reached out for a hug. "Be gentle," she said. "I'm a little banged up."

"I know the feeling." Carolina reciprocated and the two exchanged an awkward and tender embrace.

"The whole time he had me, I figured no one was looking for me. That nobody'd even notice I was gone. I had no idea that Mom or you would..."

As they broke apart, Carolina looked her over. Her face was scratched, but fine otherwise. She saw bruises on her arms though, fat, purple ones. Her lower legs, exposed below the hospital gown, were similarly discolored. A large bandage was wrapped around one calf, blood seeping through it. Her feet had countless small cuts and scrapes and her big toe was wrapped in gauze.

Despite all that, she was beautiful. Not in the sex doll sort of way that Geena was beautiful though, Scarlet's came naturally. Even her blonde hair was authentic. Carolina noticed a dime-sized piece of leaf entangled in her locks and pulled it free, staring at it.

"I know this won't be easy, but you need to tell me what happened," Carolina said. "Everything."

"Or you can save some effort and tell all of us at the same time," a voice said from the doorway.

Carolina and Scarlet both turned and saw a Pennsylvania State Trooper, his campaign hat in his hands, standing in the doorway. The man was in his forties, tall, fit. His salt and pepper hair was sheared into a high and tight and everything about his exuded all business, no personality.

"I'm Trooper Lance Cieslak with the State Police. I've been sent over to get a follow-up on your statement."

Carolina began to rise so he could have her chair, but he held up a hand. "You're fine. I can do this standing up."

"I told them everything I could remember last night," Scarlet said.

"I understand. It's routine though. Have you remembered anything else?"

Scarlet shook her head. "No, sir. It was dark. Everything was generic. Trees. Roads. There was nothing distinctive."

"You said you were held in a barn. Was it new, metal-sided? Or something older?"

"Definitely older. The farmhouse was too. It made me think of the Wyeth painting, Christina's World."

The Trooper's face clouded in confusion. Carolina wanted to tell her sister that they didn't teach art history at the academy, but decided to save that quip for later.

"Wood-sided. No paint on the boards, they'd gone gray. Two dormers on the roof," Scarlet said.

Her attention to detail impressed Carolina. Half the witnesses she'd interviewed on the job couldn't remember the color of a shirt of the man who'd held them at gunpoint.

"The bridge, the overpass from which you jumped, did it have rails or a safety barrier?"

Carolina stared at Scarlet, shocked. She jumped off a bridge?

"Just a barrier," Scarlet said.

"And you saw no street signs? No mile marker? Nothing like that?"

"I wish I had, but no. Nothing. Everything from the time I hit the truck until I came to at the gas station is a haze. The physician I saw in the E.R. said I have a concussion. I'm sorry."

"I understand." The trooper jotted all of this down. "Nothing to be sorry about. You're doing just fine."

Trooper Cieslak pocketed his pen, closed his notepad. "If

you think of anything else, here's my card." He passed one over to Scarlet. "And take it easy. You've earned a good rest."

Scarlet nodded but said nothing else.

The trooper turned and began his exit. Carolina motioned to Scarlet to hold on, then followed him out of the room. Once they were out of earshot, Carolina decided she'd bit her tongue long enough.

"Trooper Cieslak?"

He turned to face her.

"I'm Carolina McKay. Scarlet's sister. I was also a detective with the Baltimore Police. Can you fill me in on what's going on here?"

Cieslak looked like he had better places to be, but humored her. "How much do you know?"

"Only that she's been missing for over a week and what I just heard in there. So, not much."

"Okay then. I don't have a whole lot more, but here you go." He took a breath. "In Pittsburgh, on October eighteen, Miss Engle was getting in her car when she was grabbed from behind and incapacitated. How, we do not know. She did not see her assailant. She regained consciousness at a later date, chained in a barn. Another woman was being held captive at the same location. First name Eve, last name unknown. That woman was later murdered."

Carolina shuddered as she realized the horrors her sister had been through.

"During her time in confinement Miss Engle was repeatedly sexually assaulted. Last night, sometime after sunset, your sister's abductor returned with a new victim. No name for her. As the perp was restraining this new arrival, Miss Engle managed to escape. The perp chased her through a wooded area, no idea how far, until they came to a road which crossed state route two nineteen." He paused for a breath.

"With the perp bearing down on her, Miss Engle jumped

from an overpass, onto the roof of a tractor trailer which was passing below. She was knocked out by the impact. Later, when the driver stopped for gas, an employee spotted Miss Engle on the roof of his trailer via a convex mirror mounted to the building. It was then that authorities were notified. Police and rescue personnel were dispatched." He finally looked up from his notes. "And here we are."

It was a heck of an info dump, but Carolina digested all of it in bewildered amazement.

"I'm assuming a rape kit was collected?" she asked.

Cieslak nodded. "It's been sent for processing."

"Good. Will you call me as soon as you get a report?"

Another nod and Carolina gave him her cell number.

He met her gaze, connecting at a personal level for the first time. "Miss, we have no idea how many miles your sister was on the roof of that trailer. Could be hundreds. Two nineteen is a long highway that passes through multiple states. We're checking every bridge that runs over it, looking for nearby farms, but I wouldn't get your hopes up. It's quite a list and we're only getting started. Our best chance is a hit on that test."

Carolina was never one to get her hopes up, so this was par for the course. "I appreciate the information."

"Of course. It's why I'm here." He left with a nod of his head.

Carolina returned to the room to find Scarlet staring at her lap.

"What did he tell you?" Scarlet asked.

"What you told the police. Is there anything you left out or didn't want to share?"

Scarlet opened her mouth to respond, but Carolina motioned for her to wait.

"Before you answer, you should know something. In my digging to find out what happened to you, I learned what you do for a living. I'm assuming you didn't tell the police that part."

Her sister looked away and didn't answer.

Carolina sat on the side of the bed. She risked a rare attempt at affection and rested her hand over Scarlet's right. "You'll get no judgment from me. I promise. I just want to catch the fucker who did this to you."

"Isn't that what the police are for?"

"You don't want to tell the State Police about your line of work and I understand that. The Pittsburgh cops don't give a shit about sex workers. Unless they strike gold on your r—" She stopped herself. "On the DNA test, I don't have high hopes."

Scarlet furrowed her brow, worried, scared. "No, they have to find him. He's got another girl already. And there will be more."

"Then I'm going to need your full cooperation. No secrets. None."

Scarlet steeled herself, regaining some of her composure. "Of course. No secrets."

"And I might need to get a friend involved. Are you okay with that?"

Scarlet squeezed her hand with surprising strength. "Whatever it takes to find this guy is fine by me."

CHAPTER TWENTY-EIGHT

With no life threatening injuries, Scarlet was discharged from the hospital later that day and caught a ride with Carolina and Max back to her apartment. She wasted no time getting settled in.

"He barely spoke," Scarlet said after providing a physical description of the man who'd spent days torturing her. "Not because he was quiet, but because he wasn't all there."

"Wasn't all there? Like, he was crazy? A psychopath?" Carolina asked.

"No." Scarlet shook her head. "I mean, yes, he's obviously batshit insane to do the kind of shit he's doing, but that's not how I meant it. I mean..." She struggled to find the right words to get her point across.

"He never seemed to grasp the gravity of anything. Even when I broke my chains. A run-of-the-mill psycho would have been freaking out because me getting away could get him caught. He'd have been desperate to stop me. But this guy, he was playing. He could've caught me if he wanted to, I know it. But chasing me was fun."

She pulled a cigarette from a fresh pack, tapped the end against the island, then brought it to her lips and lit it. Only after a deep inhale and exhale did she continue. "It seemed like he was missing whatever part of a person makes them an adult. He was like a man-sized version of an evil child."

"You're doing great." Carolina grabbed a saucer from the kitchen cabinets and set it before Scarlet.

Scarlet tapped ash into the fine china. "I quit this almost two years ago, you know? A lot of the guys, they don't like kissing a woman who tastes like an ashtray. Guess I'm off the market for a while though." She laughed, rueful.

Carolina didn't know if her sister was actually considering a return to the lifestyle that led her to this point or if it was a crass joke. Either way she fought back a shudder.

Max had remained mostly quiet, which must have taken monumental effort from him, but he spoke then. "I've been checking the route. Backtracking from the gas station, estimating the guy was driving at sixty. That leaves about four hours that it could have been dark. Two hundred and fifty miles, give or take. And that cop was right. There are a fuck ton of overpasses on that stretch."

Carolina stared at him, raising her eyebrows, a silent way of telling him to get to the point and stop being negative.

He caught on. "So, I was wondering if you remember when he first grabbed you. Where it happened, how long you were in the car or truck or whatever, before you got to the farm."

Scarlet took a hit off the glass of wine she'd been working on, her second. Carolina knew she was on pain meds (and she hated herself for knowing the dosage and the quantity they'd given her) and that she shouldn't be drinking on top of that, but it seemed the wrong time to bring it up.

"I was supposed to meet someone. A first-time client, so we were going to meet in public, by the airport. He was highly vouched for, but I still liked to be careful. I was waiting for him in the parking lot and he was late. That pissed me off because if anyone's going to be late it should be me. So I leaned into my car to get my phone, to text him and ask him what the fuck was up. Next thing I knew, I was in a horse stall."

"How do these guys get in touch with you? Is it through Backpage or?"

Scarlet shook her head. "No. Through the app. You have to be a paying member to use it. That goes for girls and the guys. Makes it more secure. No randos."

"And what? They click your profile and send you a message like Facebook?" Max asked.

Another head shake. "No. The site's just a gallery. Any contacting is done via text. I think it's set up that way for legal reasons, so whoever runs it isn't involved in the activities of the members."

"You're going to have to explain this to me like I'm four," Carolina said. "You know technology and me don't mix. Walk me through it. Women have profiles on this app. Guys go through it like a catalog. Then what?"

Scarlet hopped down from her stool and turned toward her bedroom. "It'll be easier to show you. Let me get my iPad."

Max cleared his throat. "Um..." He grabbed it from a stand near the television.

"You found it?" she asked him. Max shook his head.

"Not me. I didn't go through your things."

That left Carolina. Scarlet looked at her and managed a smile. "I thought that was a pretty good hiding space."

"False bottom," Carolina said. "It would fool most."

"You are good at what you do." Scarlet returned to her seat, accepting the iPad from Max and flipping open the case. She scrolled off the home screen, to page two. Then she tapped an icon of a red diamond labeled JewelQuestUnlimited.

Carolina and Max exchanged a glance. Neither of them

had bothered to click on what looked like a silly, time wasting game.

When the app loaded, it was anything but. A dramatically lit black and white photo of a nude woman laying on her side, all her curves on perfect, artistic display popped onto the screen. The title at the top of the screen read No Strings Attached.

Then a pop-up box appeared. "It's been a while," Scarlet said. "I have to log in."

She did and the screen changed. Now it was a search page where you could select everything from ethnicity to location to cup size. "Once a client is registered, he or she—"

"She?" Max asked.

"Yes, hon, more than you could imagine." She continued. "He or she can start searching for the perfect match. Most probably start with location." She went to that field, typed her own zip code. That brought up a few rows of women's names.

"From there they can narrow it down further. Maybe they like blondes." She selected that option. The names changed. "Who are well endowed." She selected 32D on the menu. The photos narrowed further. Only six now.

"Did they delete your profile?" Carolina asked, already wondering if whoever was behind this app might be using it as their own personal hunting ground.

Scarlet ignored the inquiry and tapped Isabella. A second later a profile loaded, Scarlet's photos front and center. "None of us use our real names. That would be begging for trouble."

Beside Scarlet's physical stats were five golden, glowing stars out of five. A perfect score. Under that was a clickable link to Reviews. Scarlet didn't tap that and Carolina supposed she was allowed to keep some secrets.

"If a potential client likes what they see, they get your number off your photos." She clicked on one of the less risqué images. In it she wore a hot pink teddy and held a note card with her number. "Simple as that."

"You said the guy you were meeting that night was vouched for. What does that mean?"

Scarlet backtracked through the app, then tapped a small link. Vouches. "When they text you, they have to send you their ID number. You can type it in here to see if they've been with other girls and, if so, what those girls said about them. He had five or six, from what I remember. All normal. Was supposed to be a perfect gentleman."

"Only he wasn't," Carolina said, stating the obvious. Or so she thought.

"He wasn't even the same guy."

"How do you know that?"

"Because when they send their first text, they're required to send a snapshot of their driver's license along with their app ID number. It's like a two-step authentication. A low tech version, anyway. That way, if someone hacks an account, or maybe steals their buddy's ID number, you still have one more way of verifying them."

"And the guy you were meeting did this?" Carolina asked.

"He did. But it must have been someone else's license too because the guy in that picture..." She sneered. "He sure as hell wasn't the guy in the barn."

"You're not the first girl he's done this to. Maybe the monster from the barn is working with the guy on the license. Some pair of perverts like Bianchi and Buono."

Scarlet shook her head. "He's alone. There was never anyone with him at the barn."

"Maybe the guy on the license is dead," Max said. "The barn guy could have killed him, assumed his identity."

Carolina thought that sounded plausible, at least for as much sense as she could make of the process, which wasn't a lot. She felt out of the loop in this conversation and didn't like it.

It left her feeling helpless. Here she was again, a woman's life in danger, and she had no clue how to save her. Was this going to be yet another repeat of her recent failures? Was she going to have to live with more lost life on her conscience?

Max grabbed his laptop, popped the screen, inspired. "This communication, it was via your iPhone?" he asked, typing away.

"No. I use a burner for all that." Scarlet took the final puff of her cigarette, then snuffed it out on the saucer.

"Shit," Max muttered. "I thought I might be able to pull up that photo. I don't suppose you still have that burner?"

"Last time I saw it was that night."

Max shut his computer, the screen snapping down. It was about as frustrated as Carolina had ever seen him.

"Now what?" Scarlet asked.

It was a good question but none of them knew the answer. The trio was silent for a long moment, when Carolina remembered something Jack Burrell had said about nothing you do while connected to the internet being private. "Those apps, do they track the people that use them?"

"Only the shady ones," Max said, then they all paused. What could be shadier than a hookup app for escorts and johns?

"Max, can you figure out who owns that app? Maybe they have tech support or something. We need to find out if the guy that took Scarlet is still on there, contacting girls. If we're lucky—"

"Fat chance of that," Scarlet interrupted.

Carolina went on. "Maybe they can tell us where he's accessing the app from."

He shrugged. "I doubt it, but I'll see what I can dig up."

"Good." Carolina stepped away from the island, away from

them. She felt antsy, anxious, ready to crawl out of her own skin. She knew she should be relieved that her sister was alive and safe, but all she could think about was the new girl and how long she had before she was fed to the hogs.

Scarlet didn't notice anything off, but Max was more observant, or knew her better, or both.

"I know there's more going on in that head of yours, Carolina. What are you thinking?" Max asked.

"I need to talk to someone. Someone who can give me some perspective on how to find this bastard."

CHAPTER TWENTY-NINE

Max worked on his laptop while Scarlet poured a third glass of wine. Carolina had stepped into the hallway to make a phone call neither was supposed to hear. That was fine with Max. Let her handle things her way while he handled them his.

As he worked he stole glances at Scarlet, worried she might lose her mind or fall to pieces—or both—at any given moment. She'd moved on to poking around the fridge and found a half-eaten Primanti's sandwich.

"Blech," she said. "These things are revolting."

"It's an acquired taste," Max said.

"Are you talking about the sandwich or my sister?" she asked.

Max swallowed hard, shocked by her raw candor. "Umm, the, uh, food. The food."

"How did you two meet?" Scarlet moved toward him, stopping when she was across from him, only the island separating them.

He found it a challenge not to stare for too long. She was

young and gorgeous, but more than that, she reminded him of Carolina. It wasn't their looks so much as their attitudes. Their quiet confidence even when shit went bad. "We worked on a thing in Dupray. She helped me with a story."

Scarlet nodded, obviously not buying what he was selling. "And now you're just helping her out? That's quite chivalrous of you."

Max swallowed hard. "If you say so. Just friends being friends is all. That's what people do, right?"

"I've never believed men and women can be just friends. At least, not if they're both straight. It's not the way we're wired."

He tilted his head down, typing gibberish but hoping feigning work would get her to leave him alone.

"And I've most certainly never had a male friend who would drive hours and give up his life for God knows how long, without hoping to get something in return."

Damn, why couldn't she find someone else to bother? "You know, I think I get enough of the third degree from your sister. Maybe leave the interrogation to her?"

Scarlet laughed. "Oh my God. You guys banged! Or at least, you both want to."

Max's ears grew hot. He opened his mouth, ready to scramble for excuses, answers, or just mumble incoherently, but he was saved by a *ding* from the laptop. "Holy shit," he said.

"What?" Scarlet scurried around the island, tight against him as she stared at the screen.

"I just found the lead techie for the app. Teodor Stavrakis. And he's online. I'm connecting to video chat with him right now. Go get Carolina."

Scarlet left him. Max sat up in his seat, pulling his shoulders back. He licked his palm and ran his hands through his hair, smoothing the frizz.

On the screen, a chat window popped open. A man with an

unruly mane of brown hair and an equally out of control beard sat on a balcony, the ocean behind him. Shit, Max thought, cyber pimping must pay well.

"Teodor here, how can I help?"

"Hi Teodor, my name's Max."

"This is quite the change of pace from who is normally on the other end of the chat," Teodor said, his voice thick with an Eastern European accent.

"Sorry about the surprise. I'm helping a friend out with some issues," Max said.

"Ah, yes. Makes more sense. What can I help you with then?"

Carolina stepped inside, quietly shutting the door. She gave Max a nod when he glanced her way, but didn't say anything.

"There's a problem," Max said.

"What type of problem? Because if it's a billing issue I'm going to have to transfer you to—"

"No, it's not billing. It's, uh, more about customer service."

Teodor rubbed the bridge of his nose. "Ah, sorry to hear that. We pride ourselves in customer care so it's rare issues arise. Do you have a complaint?"

Carolina was beside him, slamming her hand down in front of Max and leaning into the shot. "Yeah, a big complaint. Your app is getting women killed."

Shit, Max thought. This woman has never heard the adage about files, honey, and vinegar.

Teodor was silent, his dark brown eyes wide. "Ah, miss, I... Can you repeat that?"

"Someone is using your app to kidnap and murder women. And I expect some fucking cooperation!"

Max could tell Teodor was looking back and forth between the two of them and felt the need to step in and be the mediator. "What we're hoping for is that you can help us track down a user who's suspected of multiple crimes."

Teodor looked off camera, held his hand over his mouth as he spoke to someone they couldn't see. Then his attention was back on them. "Sir, ah, I don't think that's possible. We're nothing but a glorified search engine. What our members do is of their own accord."

Carolina opened her mouth but Max put his hand over hers, trying to calm her and buy time. "I understand that," Max said. "But all we really need are IP addresses for your users who have contacted—"

Teodor looked off screen again, then back. "No, we cannot do that. Please review our TOS. It is all spelled out very explicitly that we do not—"

Carolina shoved her face into the screen. Max could only imagine how terrifying it must look on the other end of the feed. "Listen up, fuckwad. I don't give a shit about your company policy, we're talking about a serial killer who you're facilitating. Around here we call that aiding and abett—"

The feed went black and Max was certain it wasn't a connection error. He turned to Carolina, exasperated. "I track down that guy in Bulgaria of all places and you blow up on him before I can get his help."

"He wasn't going to help us." Carolina grabbed Scarlet's wine glass, took a slug. "He's a glorified Geek Squad member. We need to get the owner of that company and threaten them with the hounds of hell if that's what it takes."

Max sighed, wondering how he got himself into this. "I'll see what I can find. But maybe you could try a gentler approach next time," Max said, tired of getting trapped in dead ends.

"Yeah. There's a thought." Carolina grabbed her van keys from a bowl on the island. "I need to hit the road or I'll be late. Feel free to fuck around on the internet while I'm gone." She headed toward the door.

"You want us to go with you?" Max asked. The thought of her going anywhere in that state, in that mood, was terrifying.

She shook her head. "No, Scarlet's been through enough. I don't want her left alone."

"I'm a big girl, Carolina," Scarlet said. "And I think I proved I can handle myself."

Neither of them had realized she'd returned to the room and her presence deflated the tension.

"I'm just concerned, is all," Carolina said to her.

"I'll take care of her," Max said. "Go do whatever it is you need to do."

She left without another word and that was a relief.

CHAPTER THIRTY

So many thoughts ran through Carolina's head as she drove. But before she was able to focus on any one in particular, she popped open the pill bottle and threw two Percocets in her mouth, cracking them with her teeth and swallowing them down.

It wasn't that she was pissed at Max, she was just frustrated. Tired of banging her head against the wall. Tired of failing.

It was all leading to nowhere and Carolina hated being out of control. She was trapped in a spiral and the more she tried to stop it, the worse everything got.

She had another hour on the road and part of her wished she would have brought Max with her. But Scarlet shouldn't be alone, not yet. Not now.

And she could only imagine the ensuing questions if she'd told them about where she was headed.

Are you sure you wanna do this to yourself?

"I really don't fucking know," she answered out loud. "But I have no ideas of my own right now. Maybe he can tell me what I'm missing or where I should go."

Do you really want to open this can of worms? Can you handle this?

"Oh fuck off," Carolina said to herself. "Of course I don't. But this isn't about me. There are lives at risk and a killer on the loose. What choice do I have?"

She mentally shut down the conversation, driving the rest of the way in silence.

And she was wrong. Her own thoughts were worse than the questions anyone could ask her. She was her own worst enemy, as usual.

CHAPTER THIRTY-ONE

Carolina stood at the sign-in window for the Moundsville Hospital for the Criminally Insane. After scribbling her name, she passed her gun under the glass to an awaiting guard and walked through a metal detector which threw no alerts.

The man working guest entry—his name tag read Hoover and he looked old enough to be put out to the pasture any day now—glanced at the clipboard, then back up to Carolina. He wore the expression of someone reading a foreign language they didn't speak.

"Seriously?" he asked.

She nodded.

"This one never gets visitors. You're gonna make his day," he said, smiling.

"Somehow, I doubt that," she said.

He motioned to the folder she was carrying. "Gonna have to take a look at that."

Carolina's grip on her papers, her notes on the case so far, tightened. "Is that really necessary? It's private."

The old guard raised his eyebrows. "Got some cheesecake photos in there?" He flashed a leering grin. "Don't worry I've seen it all."

"It's not like that," she said. "It's work related."

"Still gotta look, make sure there's no contraband."

"Wouldn't the metal detector catch that?"

"Shivs and files, sure. But it don't catch drugs."

Carolina furrowed her brow. "Do I really look like a drug addict?"

He examined her and she thought maybe she'd pressed her luck too far that time. "You'd be surprised the people," he said. "Now hand it over."

She did and he paged through with little interest. Once he was satisfied there were no hidden joints or baggies of smack, he returned it to her. "Head up to that next door on the right. Pamela'll take care of you."

Following his directions, she went to the next door and pressed a small buzzer. The door opened and a female guard, one too young and too pretty to work in a place like this, led her down a stark white hallway. The place had zero personality or character and felt cold even though the heat was running and it was at least seventy.

They approached a set of double doors which opened to something akin to a courtyard. The female guard opened the door on the right and waved her through. "Make yourself comfortable," she said. "We'll bring him out."

In this makeshift park, shrubbery added color but the trees were bare. A few men in maroon jumpsuits shuffled about aimlessly. One had a handful of bread which he fed to a fat squirrel. All of the men looked tired and worn out, but none looked crazy.

Not that crazy had a look. If it did, her life would have been much less traumatic.

She slouched on a vacant, green bench and waited. Her

eyes went to a bird feeder, filed to the brim with millet, cracked corn, and wheat. Apparently the state couldn't spring for sunflower seeds, cheap bastards. A chickadee and a nuthatch shared space at the feed and she watched them as she waited for a long five minutes.

Then a steel door clanged open. Her body went tense in anticipation, worry, and guilt. Her leg began to shake and she wanted to get up and run the other direction. Instead, she turned to the door.

He gripped the handrail like it was a life preserver as he descended three concrete steps, eyes glued to his feet to ensure stable footing. He hadn't seen her yet, but even at twenty yards his handsome face stood out to her. She almost smiled, but the jumpsuit spoiled the sight. He shouldn't have to wear that damned thing, she thought, wishing she could see him one more time in his sheriff's uniform.

When Lester Fenech hit ground level his gaze drifted straight ahead for the first time. Immediately he found Carolina and his tentative, worried face transformed into one filled with unabated joy.

"Carolina!" he called out. The doddery, old man who'd looked afraid to walk now broke into a jog as he hurried to her.

"I don't know the protocol here," Carolina said. "Am I allowed to hug you or—"

"I don't give a good goddamn if it's allowed or not," he said.

Lester wrapped his strong arms around her, and she was transported back to the world of a twelve-year-old girl when he was her surrogate father and life was good and far less complicated. Why couldn't they have frozen time back then?

"How are you doing, Lester?" Carolina asked, feeling the tears build up in her eyes, but she refused to let that dam break.

He rubbed her back, then released her. "Oh, they say I have more good days than bad ones, which I suppose is progress. Though, I don't remember much of the bad ones."

"You look good," she said and she meant it. She'd worried she'd arrive to find him doped up and drooling on the floor. Aside from the jumpsuit, he looked like the same man she's always known and loved.

He patted his belly which had expanded some since she'd last seen him. "I eat better here than I did as a bachelor."

"Well, I'm glad they're taking good care of you."

He nodded and there was a brief, uncomfortable lull.

"I need you to know that what happened back at the cabin, I wasn't myself. I'd never hurt you if everything up here," he pointed to his skull, "was firing right."

She put her hand on his chest. "I know," she offered. "But we don't need to talk about it."

"I thought maybe that's why you came. To read me the riot act. I wouldn't blame you either. My doctor here, her name's Chandran, she's Indian. She says it's important to get your feelings out and not bottle everything up inside. If I'd have done that back when—" He shook his head. "Never mind. We can do that some other time."

Lester waved his hands around the courtyard. "What brings you all the way to Moundsville? Certainly not the scenery."

"I need your advice. Your professional expertise."

"About what?" he asked.

"Catching a serial killer."

CHAPTER THIRTY-TWO

"My Lord," Lester said after a long moment of silence.

She had told him everything, not holding back on even the grimiest of details. As she'd told the story she wondered if this would be too much for him. If it could trigger his alter to return, but he took it all in with the patience and understanding he'd displayed throughout decades of public service.

Among the info were photos Max had texted her during her drive to Moundsville. Scarlet had contacted Geena and they pulled images of the two other missing escorts from the NoStringsAttached app. Their stage names were Sapphire and Felicity.

Lester had those photos laid out beside Scarlet's, creating something of a timeline.

"Do you know when these first women disappeared?" he asked.

"Within the last three or four weeks."

"He's working fast then. If I had to guess, I'd say there were others earlier on. Guys like this don't usually move so quick out of the gate. They need to work up to it."

He paged through the notes but couldn't find what he was looking for. "The woman he killed in front of Scarlet, I think you said her name was Eve?"

Carolina nodded.

"Did she know how long Eve was there before her?"

"Scarlet said she was pretty out of it. She thought it was a little over a week."

"And Scarlet was held for nine days before she escaped. That's also when the newest woman was brought in. So, it seems like, after a week and a half, he gets bored with them." He looked up at her. "He's like a kid who gets tired of his new toys a week after Christmas and throws a tantrum until he gets a new one."

Carolina knew he was right about that. And it jived with Scarlet's comments about how it seemed like a game to the killer. "That means the new girl, she's got ten days, maybe twelve, if she's lucky."

Lester ran his fingers through his long, thinning hair, pushing it off his face. "And he seems to prefer two at a time. So he'll be hunting again. Soon, if he's not already."

"Shit," Carolina said. She could almost hear the clock ticking down in her head and the weight of the responsibility was firmly on her shoulders.

"I've got to stop this, Lester. The Pittsburgh cops aren't interested. And there are too many jurisdictional roadblocks to get the State Police involved quick. This is on me."

He sighed, an exasperated noise that sounded the way Carolina felt. "This isn't your responsibility, Carolina. You need to be careful about bearing too many burdens."

She appreciated the words, but couldn't accept them. "If not me, then who?" She checked her watch, shocked with how much time had passed. It would be dark soon and the temperature outside had turned near frigid. "I should go before you freeze to death out here," she said to him.

He chuckled. "I've survived worse."

Wasn't that the truth?

She began to regather the paperwork, but he stopped her, putting his aged-spotted hand atop the photos.

"Did Scarlet give a physical description of Eve and the new woman?"

Carolina tried to think back to what Scarlet had told her. "She said the new girl was beautiful. Busty. Tall. She didn't say much about Eve, just that she was in really rough shape."

"How about hair color?"

"The new one was blonde. I think Eve might have been too. Do you want me to text her and check?"

Lester shook his head. "That's unnecessary." He tapped each of the faces on the photograph, slow and deliberate.

"I know you see what I see," he said.

She looked them over and, of course, he was right. The two missing escorts and Scarlet all had long, blonde hair, strikingly beautiful faces, bodies to die for.

"That's his type," Carolina said.

"Sure is." Lester shuffled the photos into the stack, done with them. "And whoever he targets next, she'll check those boxes too."

It wasn't much, but it was something. When she got back to Pittsburgh they could get on the app and search for girls who fit the profile, alert them to what was happening. But how would that save the one who was already chained in the barn?

"How do I catch this fucker?" she asked, both to Lester and herself.

Behind them the steel door clanked. A guard stepped out, immediately tucking his hands into his armpits to stave off the cold. "About time to head inside, Fenech," he said. "Tell your daughter to come back some other time."

Neither of them corrected him.

"Alright, Robbins. I'm on my way." He stood, stretching out joints which had stiffened from sitting too long in the cool, October temperatures.

"Thank you, Lester." Carolina gave him a hug this time, but it was quick lest the guard decide to cop an attitude. "This has helped."

"I wish I could do more," he said, and his eyes shined, avid and eager. A lawman's eyes. Some things never went away.

"And I will be back. Soon. I promise."

He smiled, but this one was full of sadness and regret. He wasn't ready for this visit to end. Neither was she.

"Get to stepping, pops," the guard called.

Lester turned away from her, moving toward the guard. She held her files tight against her chest and watched him take a few steps, then moved toward the opposite exit.

She was almost there when his voice called across the courtyard.

"Carolina?"

She turned back to him. "A guy like this, there's only two ways you'll ever get him," Lester said.

"I'd settle for one."

"You could catch him in the act, but finding his little torture farm sounds unlikely from what you've told me. It would take a lot of rocks being turned over, and a lot of time. More than that woman has, I reckon."

"What's my second option?" she asked.

"Lure him out. Nab him while he's trying to take a new woman. That'll most likely be soon."

It sounded good in theory, but... "What do we lure him with?"

"Elven ever tell you about how he taught me to fish?"

She smiled, recalling the photo of Elven and Lester at some river out west. "He did."

"Most important lesson he gave me was that catching the big fish is all about finding the perfect bait. For salmon, you want a flasher with a hoochie. Trout, they like a vibrax spinner. For bass, especially the trophy ones, you want a good jig and a trailer."

He looked back to the guard who had shifted from genial to glaring and took a couple steps in the man's direction to placate him, then turned one last time to Carolina.

"You already know what your fellow bites on. To catch the perfect killer, you need the perfect victim."

CHAPTER THIRTY-THREE

Carolina rushed into the condo, wired despite the drive. All the way back she formulated her plan, perfecting the steps she was going to take to catch the monster.

She was going to become the bait.

She would be the perfect victim.

It had come together perfectly in her head and she was excited to tell Scarlet and Max, but when she entered the apartment Scarlet was nowhere to be seen and Max was asleep on the couch. So much for a welcome home party. But, after the way she'd left, she couldn't blame them.

In checking Scarlet's bedroom, she found her curled on the bed, legs tucked, arms wrapped around them. She looked small, almost childlike. At first, Carolina thought her sister was asleep, but then she heard sniffling. And soft, barely there sobs.

Her good mood crashed down around her.

Scarlet had seemed wounded, but stable at the hospital. And when they got back to the apartment she was checked in and eager to help answer any questions they had. Only now that the initial rush of her escape had passed, reality was hitting her. Surviving the ordeal wasn't even half the battle. Now she had to find a way to climb back.

Seeing her sister laying there, balled in a fetal position while she cried made Carolina more determined than ever to make this plan work.

She'd catch this bastard or die trying.

After backing away from Scarlet's bedroom, she went to the couch where Max was sawing a forest's worth of logs and gently shook him.

"Max?"

His snore broke into a sputter, but then resumed.

"Max? Wake up." She gave him another, less gentle shake and that time his eyelids fluttered.

"Damn," he said, his voice froggy. "What time is it?"

"A little after eight. You two turned in early."

He sat up, covering his mouth as he yawned. "Guess the adrenaline wore off," he said.

Carolina tilted her head toward the bedroom. "How is she?"

Max frowned. "Not so hot. I think it's catching up with her. After you left, she drained that bottle of wine and went for another, but I stopped her. Told her it wasn't smart with her meds."

"How'd she take that?"

"How do you think?"

"That well, huh?"

He nodded. "Worse. She called me a few rather creative expletives, then stormed off to her room. Hasn't talked to me since. That was about four hours ago." He blinked a few times, clearing sleep from his eyes. "Where'd you go anyway?"

"To see Lester."

The name snapped him wide awake. "Say again, because I know what I think I just heard can't be true."

"He was sick. You know that."

"He tried to murder us."

"Fuck off with that. At least for the time being. Despite what he's been through, he's still the best cop I've ever known."

Max rolled his eyes. "Says a lot."

She dodged the jab. "I talked to him about the case. And he helped me figure out what we need to do next."

"And what's that?" Max asked.

She knew he wasn't going to like this, so she decided to break it to him piecemeal. "Well, to start I need you to go to the department store."

"For what?"

"Bleach."

Confusion clouded his face. "She probably had some if we look around."

"No, not that kind of bleach. The kind you use on hair."

SINCE BLEACH WASN'T EXACTLY specific and because Carolina knew as much about coloring hair as she did college football, she decided to roll the dice and get Scarlet involved in this transformation. Neither her sister nor Max wanted anything to do with the plan, asserting that it was too dangerous and too stupid, but Carolina wouldn't be deterred.

Scarlet worked up a list of products and Max headed to the nearest Target to retrieve them. During his absence, Carolina attempted to have an awkward heart to heart with the sister she barely knew. It involved a lot of crying, cursing, and one thrown dinner plate.

Carolina listened to all the hurt and anger and fear and guilt come out. She knew this was just the beginning, but as the conversation petered out, Scarlet seemed in marginally better spirits. She even expressed an appetite. When Carolina suggested they get pizza delivered her sister laughed in her face and, for once, her shameless snobbery was welcome.

Scarlet called one of her favorite high-end restaurants where she was apparently a regular, and asked them to deliver a variety of food Carolina couldn't even pronounce. It arrived about the same time that Max returned.

"I didn't know this was a party," Max said, dropping a shopping bag full of hair care products onto the island.

"That's because we weren't going to invite you," Scarlet said.

Max and Carolina exchanged a quick nod. She's back.

As they ate Carolina stripped down to her bra so Scarlet could apply the first round of bleach to her hair. It smelled horrendous and Max asked at least three times if this was going to make her hair fall out. Scarlet promised it wouldn't, but even Carolina was skeptical.

Two hours later, and a round of something called purple shampoo, she looked at herself in the bathroom mirror and wanted to throw up her dinner. She was blonde. And she hated it.

Hate wasn't a strong enough word. Loath, detest, abhor. She longed for a thesaurus to find the most extreme word possible.

"You look amazing," Scarlet said from behind her.

Carolina scowled at her sister's reflection. "Bullshit. I look like I should be cashing in my Camel Cash for a new windbreaker."

That made Scarlet laugh and as horrified as Carolina was by her appearance, the laughter almost made it worthwhile.

"It just needs styled. You wait." She turned Carolina away from the mirror so she couldn't follow along, grabbed a curling iron, and went to work.

When she finished, Scarlet still refused to let her see

herself. "No. We need an unbiased third party," Scarlet said. "Max? Come here."

After some footsteps, he stood outside the closed door. "I'm not just walking in there. You have to invite me. Like a vampire."

Scarlet moved to the door. "Close your eyes," she instructed, before opening it.

Max chewed his lips. "Last time I heard that from two women, I opened them to a ransacked dorm room and my wallet was missing."

"Believe me, I don't need your money," Scarlet said and Max did as told.

Her sister motioned for Carolina to stand. But what she wanted to do was fade into the walls. What had made her think she could pull this off? Or, at the least, why hadn't she just bought a wig?

When Carolina was at Scarlet's side, it was time for the big reveal.

"Okay, open them," Scarlet said.

Max did, flinching involuntarily when he saw Carolina's new do. "Holy shit!"

Carolina spun to her sister. "I told you! I look like a freak."

"No you don't," Max said. "It's just... Holy shit," he repeated. "You look like a different person."

"Good different?" Carolina asked.

He paused, carefully selecting his words. "I've never been into the Barbie thing," he said, then took a shameful glance at Scarlet. "No offense." Back to Carolina. "But it works somehow. I didn't think it would, but it does."

"You're just saying that so I don't take my pistol and blow my brains out."

Max shook his head and she could see in his eyes he was being honest. "I'm not. You look like a Bond villain or something. It's kind of hot. But, Carolina, I think you're a smokeshow no matter the color of your hair."

Carolina had been standing there in her bra and jeans without a care, but was suddenly self-conscious and wrapped her arms around herself for cover. "If you say so."

"I do," Max said, grinning.

"Okay, show's over," Scarlet said, pushing against his chest. "Go back to whatever you were doing, but if you're going to squeeze one out, don't use my good hand towels, okay?"

If a black man could blush, Max did, then he made a hasty retreat.

The two women looked at one another. "Now what?" Carolina said.

"To my bedroom. It's time for your photoshoot."

SCARLET DIPPED INTO HER CLOSET, sorting through her lingerie. She emerged with a sheer, black teddy composed of less material than a sock.

"Oh, hell no," Carolina said.

"Yeah," Scarlet said. "We can do better." She rummaged, muttering aloud. "Nothing white. You're too pale for that. And not blue. It'll clash with your eyes..."

Hangers scraped against the rods, more muttering, most of it unintelligible. "Yes," Scarlet said. "This."

She popped out of the closet holding a royal purple satin corset and matching panties.

It looked like something that belonged on a pin-up model, or Scarlet, not herself. "Don't you have like, a bodysuit?"

"You're not getting hits on the app in a bodysuit. Trust me, this one is perfect for you. Your tits will look stupendous."

Carolina sighed, resigned to feeling like a fraud and looking like a fool. But the sooner this part was over, the sooner she could get back to business. And, if everything went as planned, to being her real self.

"Fine. Give it to me," she said, snatching it from her sister. "Go get your camera, or phone, whatever you used for your photos."

"I hired a professional photographer. I flew up to New York City for the shoot. He shot the Pirelli calendar a few years ago."

Carolina forced herself not to roll her eyes. "Well, I'm not doing that. So figure out a way to make this work."

Scarlet smirked and left the room, leaving Carolina alone.

She held the outfit in front of herself, staring at her reflection in the mirror. Who was this stranger looking back at her?

CHAPTER THIRTY-FOUR

The afternoon of the following day, her profile went live on NoStringsAttached. Her new name was Jezebel—Scarlet's suggestion—and all they could do was wait and hope.

As the hours passed, a niggling seed of worry sprouted and grew in Carolina's mind. She was used to going rogue, to skirting the boundaries of what was legal and occasionally vaulting over that line if the situation demanded it. But that was in West Virginia, where she had backup. Where Lester or Elven had her back and could cover for her if she went too far off the rails.

Now she was in a new state, one where the police were not only unhelpful, but downright dismissive of her and her concerns. What if she went out to meet a prospective john only to encounter an undercover cop? Even if they believed her story, this vigilante act wouldn't be well-received. And if she ended up in jail, even temporarily, all of this was for naught as the killer would remain on the loose and more women would die.

Her leg shook so hard the table where she sat, overlooking

Pittsburgh's banal cityscape, rattled. She thought she was alone, but Max's voice disproved that.

"It's not too late to stop this," he said.

She spun to face him.

"Well, I guess the hair thing is," he added. "But not the rest."

That brought a weak smile. "No, this is what needs done, Max."

He sat across from her, elbows on the table, hands pressed together, tenting his fingers. "This might be news to you, Carolina, but it's not your responsibility to single handedly bring every killer in the world to justice."

"What's the alternative? Sit here twiddling my thumbs while another innocent girl dies? Meanwhile Scarlet gets to live with the knowledge that the guy who abducted and raped her is still out there?"

Max had been literally twiddling his thumbs and stopped. "There are police for a reason," Max said.

"Yeah, police who don't give a fuck about sex workers."

"But why go it alone?" he asked.

"I'm not alone. I have you."

He sighed. "I appreciate the confidence, but you can do better. Maybe I can blindside a pothead, but you need people with experience backing you up. Don't you have any friends from Baltimore who would help you?"

She ran through her list of colleagues she could count on from her days employed by the Baltimore P.D. That took all of half a second. "No."

"There isn't anyone out there in law enforcement who owes you a favor? Because, if there is, it's time to call it in."

She racked her brain, trying to recall everyone she'd crossed paths with over the last fifteen years. When she finally came up with a name, it was from much more recent history.

"You still have that business card I gave you at Downtown Pawn?" she asked.

Max pulled out his wallet, rifled through the contents, and extracted it. He set it on the table between them. "Jack Burrell, professional fuckup."

Carolina leaned into the table. "What's that mean?"

"I was bored yesterday while you were gone. Did a deep dive into his career history for shits and giggles."

"What did you find?"

"Nothing good. Dude used to be on the murder squad with the FBI but got himself in a heap of trouble over a serial killer case in Buffalo. Local police had a suspect in for questioning, but Burrell said he didn't fit the profile and to let him go. That same guy killed three more women before they caught him elbows deep in a college student."

"Fuck..." Carolina said.

"Yeah. That," Max said. "Anyway, after that he almost got bounced from the bureau, but he knew somebody and managed to stay employed. Got downgraded to financial crimes though, somewhere his fool ass couldn't get anyone else killed."

Carolina pressed her index finger against Jack's business card and slid it to herself. She picked it up, examined it. "Well, he's still better than nothing," she said.

Max crossed his arms, displeased. "I'm not so sure about that."

CHAPTER THIRTY-FIVE

"Fascinating," Jack said, chomping into a cheesesteak loaded down with onions and oozing Cheez Whiz. "She's one lucky lady."

Carolina sat across from him, in the same booth they'd occupied only days before. She was surprised he was still in the city. 'Paperwork,' he'd stated as the reason. But when she called he sounded bored and when she offered to buy him dinner, he didn't hesitate to accept.

She'd tucked her newly blonde locks under a knit slouch hat Scarlet had provided, not wanting to answer what would have been his first question out of the gate otherwise. He seemed to notice nothing different and devoured his food as she told him about Scarlet's ordeal and the recent developments. That section of the conversation had reached its finale and she was at the part where she needed to grovel for his help.

Carolina was glad she'd chewed two Percocets down before the meeting. "She is. But the girl being held captive in the psycho's barn... She's not so lucky."

Jack nodded, used a napkin to wipe Whiz from his mouth,

then shrugged. "State PoPo are on it," he said. "They're good eggs." He finished the remains of his second shake with one long suck.

"They are. But you know how slow things move when you're jumping jurisdictions. The girl, she probably doesn't have that long."

Jack frowned, considering that. "You want the FBI to get involved," he said. "That's why you called me. And here I thought you were just being nice." He began to gather together his empty dishes. "Well, I'm a good guy despite what you might have called me the other morning. And I'll be happy to make a couple calls. But, unless state lines have been crossed, the Bureau can't get involved until invited by a local agency. You'll have to get someone working your sister's case to—"

"Jack, I don't want the FBI's help. I want yours."

He stayed silent for a while, folding his used napkin into an even square and depositing it on the stack of plates and silverware. With his food finished, he pulled a lollipop from his jacket pocket and used it to satiate his oral fixation.

"What am I supposed to do? I'm in financial fraud. Purely white collar, low stakes matters."

"I know. And I know what you used to do at the agency."

Jack leaned back in his booth, hands folded on the table, a sour expression crossing his narrow face. "Sounds like you've been looking into me. And depending on what you say next, I might bring what has been a very cordial until this point dinner conversation to an end. How do you plan to proceed, Carolina McKay?"

It was her turn to take a beat, to plan her words. "I hoped you would consider helping me on this because I respect you and trust you. I don't care about your past. I really believe that we can nail this bastard if we work together."

Some of the sourness left his face. "And what's in it for me?

Other than a nice meal and friendly conversation with a pretty lady?"

"Maybe redemption? Your chance to show everyone you're still a quality agent, one capable of catching killers." She leaned into the table, her eyes locked on his. "Jack, if we pull this off, it's proof to the agency that *they're* the fuckups."

Jack pulled the lollipop from his mouth, twirled it with his slender fingers. "I have always found spite to be a fine motivator."

"Does that mean you'll help?"

"I have three weeks of unused vacation. And this sounds more interesting than that golf trip I had planned in Boca."

Carolina grinned and held her fist across the table. Jack caught on quick and bumped it with his own.

"I appreciate that, Jack," she said. "I'll call you as soon as we have a lead."

CHAPTER THIRTY-SIX

CAROLINA SAT AT THE ISLAND AND WATCHED SCARLET. She was sprawled on the couch, glass of wine in reach, looking at but not watching the TV as some daytime drama droned on.

She was worried about her sister. Maybe even more worried now than when she'd been missing. Scarlet had been violently attacked and raped. She'd seen a woman die. Carolina hadn't lived through that exact trauma, but she knew that such an ordeal causes scars that never healed. You just had to find a way to live with them.

Max was gone, at the store buying groceries, but he left his iPad behind and it gave a cheerful ding. Scarlet bolted upright, knocking her glass of red off the coffee table, the wine saturating the white throw rug beneath it. She paid it no attention, rushing to Carolina's side as she opened the tablet.

"You do it," Carolina said, still wary of technology and afraid she'd press a wrong button. They were waiting for the same john, the same driver's license photo, to show up. Scarlet was certain she'd recognize it, and Carolina believed her, but she worried nonetheless about her sister getting too deeply involved in the investigation.

Scarlet tapped the screen, opened the texts, read the new message, stared at the photo.

"Fuck," Scarlet muttered, spinning toward the wine bottle nearby.

As her sister grabbed her fallen glass to refill it, Carolina examined the text message. The driver's license showed a guy in his forties with a perfect Van Dyke, a round face, and a rapidly receding hairline. Not their guy. Again.

"I was sure it would be him this time." Scarlet took a slug of wine.

Carolina shifted her attention from the tablet to her sister. "Why?"

Scarlet shrugged. "Because I think every text is going to be the one. Instead, they're just regular, non-homicidal guys looking to have fun. Hell, a few of them were my regulars."

"Really?" Carolina asked.

"Your profile is getting a lot of attention," Scarlet said. "They like you."

Carolina huffed. Yeah right.

"Don't scoff," Scarlet said. "You could make a good living at this."

Carolina appreciated the intent, if not the compliment itself. "Thanks, but I don't think it's the lifestyle for me."

She didn't need to remind her sister where escorting had got her, and Scarlet's pretty face sagged.

"Don't worry," Carolina said. "He'll bite soon. Guys like him, they can't help themselves."

Scarlet chewed her lip, her skepticism obvious. "Maybe he already found someone," Scarlet said. "What if the reason he hasn't responded yet is because he filled his quota of two. And if we do eventually get a hit, it could be because the girl I left there, when I ran, is dead."

Carolina stood, moving closer to her sister. She wanted to reach out, to show some sort of affection, but it always felt awkward and forced. The best she could do was a clumpy pat on the shoulder. "None of this is your fault. We're going to find him, alright?"

Scarlet nodded, still sniffling.

Before either could say more, the doorknob jiggled, the door rattling in its frame. Scarlet flinched, trembling all over.

"Man with his arms full," Max said through the closed door. "A little help would be welcome."

His voice return broke the moment, if there had ever been one, and Scarlet slipped to the door, unlocking it. Carolina knew, if they didn't get a solid lead soon, the facade of having her shit together that Scarlet had created was going to crumble. She didn't know if her excessive drinking was a new problem, but she'd heard Scarlet crying herself to sleep each night. Most days she seemed in a trance, or in shock.

Carolina had even spotted the box for an over-the-counter STD test in the bathroom trash can, but hadn't broached that subject yet.

As she watched Scarlet and Max unload the grocery bags and put the items in their proper places, she said a silent prayer and she didn't care who was listening. At this point, she'd make a deal with the Devil if that's what it took.

CHAPTER THIRTY-SEVEN

The Devil came calling three hours later.

"I'll be motherfucked," Scarlet said, staring at the snapshot of the driver's license.

"Is it him?" Carolina asked, but her sister's voice had answered the question before it was even asked.

The man in the driver's license was in his sixties with stylishly cut salt and pepper hair. He wore a suit jacket and tie and both looked expensive. He was just short of handsome, falling into the distinguished category, and looked like he might work in upper management at a bank or law firm. Maybe even an executive.

"It is," Scarlet said. "Well, I mean, it's not *him*. Not the monster, but it's the ID he sent me."

"Screenshot that shit," Max said from behind them, as he stared at the screen. "Then send it to me. I want that backed up on as many devices as we got."

The three of them stared at the photo, taking in every detail of the man. In the photo, a nickel covered the personal details on the license. But at the edge of the frame was a partial address. No town, but the street. 1953 Sequo— The remainder was cut off.

"Max, see if you can find anything on—"

"On it," he said, his thoughts aligning with her own. He grabbed his laptop and began searching.

After the photo, a message had been sent.

You are sublime. Would love to meet.

Scarlet worked the tablet, typing a response.

"What are you doing?" Carolina asked, nerves setting in. This was happening. Part of her thought the plan would never come to fruition.

"Answering him," Scarlet said. "We don't want him to think you're not interested and move on to someone else. These guys have short attention spans."

She watched Scarlet's message appear on the screen.

Hey Hon. Thanks 4 the interest. U looking 4 all nite or?

Carolina checked Max. "Anything yet?"

"It's not a lot to work on," he said. "Give me a—"

She didn't hear his answer because a reply came through.

All night and then some. The longer the better. Then a wink emoji.

Scarlet responded.

Good things don't come cheap. I'm a high class girl with expensive tastes...

"Shit," Max muttered and both women looked to him.

"What?"

"I got a hit," he said.

"That's a good thing, right?" Scarlet asked.

"Not really. I'm sure it's Sequoia but don't know if it's road, street, lane, avenue. Between all of those we're looking at dozens of potential matches. And that's just in Allegheny County."

He spun the laptop around and showed the screen. There were countless dots on the map. So much for that brilliant idea.

A new response came.

That's okay. $$$$$ is no object.

Then he sent a photo of a fanned-out splay of cash. All hundred dollar bills. Three thousand, at least.

So when? I need to know so I can get ready.

"Ask him if he wants to meet at his place," Carolina told Scarlet. "Then tell him you need the address."

"That's doubtful," Scarlet said. "Almost all of the clients are married. Unless his wife is out of town..."

"Try it."

Scarlet did.

Your place or mine?

They waited.

"Max, can you see if any of those addresses go along with a farm? Or if they're in the vicinity of a farm?" Carolina asked.

"I'll check."

My place is off limits. Hotel.

"Damn it." Carolina tried to focus, tried to think of the perfect question, but she came up blank.

"What should I tell him?" Scarlet asked.

Carolina felt her leg shaking. She yearned for a pill or two. Or three.

"Tell him that's fine. You—I mean I—can meet him tonight."

Scarlet looked to her, mouth pinched with worry. "Are you sure? What about that FBI guy? Can he even make it tonight?"

Carolina had no idea. "Just do it."

Scarlet typed.

Tonight works. Got a hotel in mind? I like the Marriott downtown.

"Nothing's jumping out at me," Max said. "Most of these addresses are in the suburbs."

Carolina hadn't expected a miracle but was still frustrated. Nothing could ever be easy. She clenched her fists so tight she thought she might carve gashes in her palms. The tablet dinged. Her answer had come.

Can't tonight. Not ready. Tomorrow @7?

She exhaled hard even though she hadn't been aware she was holding her breath. She wanted to get this over with, but felt a surge of relief at the delay. "Yes, tell him yes. That works."

Scarlet did.

A second later came the response.

Can't wait! Wear red. My favorite color. Celtic Inn near Greensburg. Will text the room when you're here. 7pm. Do not be late.

"We're in," Carolina said, knowing they had him. And they had time to do it the right way.

But when she turned to Scarlet, prepared to celebrate, tears streamed down her sister's face and dripped onto her chest.

"What's wrong?" Carolina asked.

"Nothing." Scarlet wiped at her eyes. "Everything. I... It's just knowing he's still out there. The way he sounds so fucking excited. I don't... I can't—"

Scarlet bounced out of her chair, sprinting to the bathroom, slamming the door closed. Through it, Carolina heard her retching and sobbing.

She felt like crying herself, but wouldn't allow it. Instead she funneled all that sadness a different direction and used it to fuel her growing rage.

CHAPTER THIRTY-EIGHT

After the exchange she called Jack and filled him in. He had taken his vacation days and said he was ready to help, so they agreed to meet at the apartment at four p.m. the next day to plan out what would follow.

Scarlet spent nearly an hour in the bathroom and when she finally came out she seemed worn out and hollow. She went straight to her bedroom without a word.

Carolina was spent too. The adrenaline had worn off and she just wanted to sleep. Well, take some pills, and sleep. And that's exactly what she did.

After waking the next morning she knew she couldn't sit in the apartment all day. Doing so would send her over the edge and she needed her wits about her. She had to go into this cool and prepared. And there was only one person who could steady her nerves.

"I could get used to these visits," Lester said.

He looked so happy to see her, but Carolina could barely conjure a smile in return. She couldn't get Scarlet out of her mind. Couldn't stop thinking about the girl still—hopefully—chained up in the barn being raped on the regular and awaiting a savage death, her corpse to become hog feed.

"We got the guy," she said.

He sat beside her on the bench, put his hand over hers. "Well, that's great. So why do you look like someone ran over your favorite cat?"

She'd debated how much to tell him during the drive to Moundsville, ultimately deciding on everything. And that's what she did. Pouring out her emotions, telling him how wrecked Scarlet was, how worried she was this guy would get away and keep killing.

She didn't cry—crying is for sissies, as her mother always admonished—but she let him put his arm around her and steady her as she shook. He didn't say a word, only listening and letting her put it all on the table.

By the time she was finished, her voice was hoarse, her mouth dry. But she had one more thing to say.

"Lester, I need to confess something. I guess it's preemptive, but you're the only person in the whole world I think will understand what I'm going to tell you."

He stared at her with his kind, sad eyes. "You can tell me anything, hon. I won't judge."

And she knew he wouldn't. "When I find the guy who's doing this, I'm going to kill him."

Saying the words aloud made her feel fifty pounds lighter. She knew it was an awful thing to want, to plan. It went against everything that had made her a cop. Against everything that made a person good and moral. But it was going to happen anyway.

"I know where that feeling comes from," he said. "I lived it. You know that."

She nodded. It was Lester's own need for vengeance that destroyed his life and mental health. But his cautionary tale didn't deter her.

"I don't know if your mind is set, but I wish you'd reconsider. I think your plan to catch him is a fine one, but you let that FBI fellow take him into custody. Let the courts deal with him, and believe me they will. He'll spend his days where he can't hurt other women and you'll be able to live out yours with a clean conscience."

She'd expected this. It's what a good father would do and even though Lester Fenech wasn't her father by blood, he was in every other way that mattered. "But he needs to be punished," she said. "He doesn't deserve to live after what he's done."

Lester looked past her, to the birdfeeder where a mourning dove had squeezed its plump, gray body onto an undersized perch. "Nothing can undo what's been done. I know that first hand." He turned his gaze back to her, his own eyes threatening with tears as he studied her face.

And then he smiled. It was the most tender, compassionate smile she'd ever seen.

"I see a lot of myself in you, Carolina Wren. And I want you to know that, no matter what, I'll always love you."

She fell into him then, and felt his chest hitch as he cried. Somehow, she held herself together. "Thank you, Lester. For everything. I love you too."

CHAPTER THIRTY-NINE

Jack was already at the apartment when Carolina returned, pacing from one end of the windows to the next. He nearly jumped out of his cheap suit when she threw open the door.

"Where were you?" Jack asked.

"Good to see you too," she said, already put on edge by his tone. "And I was visiting a friend. Not that it's any of your business."

He strode her way, yanking the lollipop from his mouth and pointing it at her like a sixth finger. "This half-assed plan you cobbled together all hinges on you, and you disappear for half a day for what, old home week?"

"First of all, fuck you. Second, I told you to meet at four. It's not even three thirty."

Jack checked his watch and some of the righteous indignation left him. "Oh."

"Yeah. Oh." She dropped her keys onto the counter. Max was on his computer, as usual. Scarlet half-asleep on the couch. What a motley crew we are, she thought.

Scarlet sat up, then looked on the verge of toppling over. She wasn't just tipsy, she was drunk. "To the bedroom," she said. "I have to get you ready."

Carolina followed her staggering sister. The outfit Scarlet had chosen for her, a tight, skimpy red dress, laid on the bed. "Isn't there something with a bit more... coverage?" Carolina asked.

"The guy had expectations," Scarlet said. "You show up in jeans and he'll know something's weird."

It's just one night, Carolina told herself. A few hours. I can do this.

Jack stood in the doorway, arms crossed over his chest as he watched. "We need to talk."

"It can wait five minutes." Carolina closed the door in his face and began undressing.

A few minutes later she was poured into the dress, felt awkward as hell, and was ready to get this mess over with. She opened the bedroom door and stepped into the main area. Predictably, Jack and Max stared, Jack not even bothering to close his mouth.

"You two get a good enough look?" Carolina asked.

Max grinned, but Jack stammered. "I, uh."

"Get the blood back to your head, Jack. We've got a killer to catch," Carolina said.

"Speaking of," Jack began, "I'm going to reach out to my contacts at the Pittsburgh PD. Bring them in on this."

"The hell you are. Those pricks had their chance to help and had no interest."

"When you asked for my help, I thought we were talking about running background checks."

Carolina had lied to the man, but wasn't ready to accept responsibility. "It got more complicated," she said. "How was I supposed to know the guy would want to meet so soon?"

"That's exactly the point," Jack said. "You told me that we wouldn't be doing anything dangerous."

"He's got a point, Carolina." Max tapped his finger against his computer, a nervous tic. "You know I'm always on board for a Scooby Doo caper, but this is a real mean son of a bitch we're dealing with. What if something goes wrong and we spook him? He could run and start over, doing this somewhere else. Is that what you want?"

"That's why I got Jack involved. The professionals are going to handle this." She shot Jack a peeved glance. "You can still do that, can't you Jack? Work a real case?"

He leaned against the wall and she could almost see the gears turning in his head. "Here's a question for you," Jack said. "You and I go there and the john shows up, but he's not going to look like the guy in the driver's license, because we're assuming that's stolen, correct?"

Carolina nodded.

"How do you know the john that contacted you is the same psycho john that is committing these crimes? I mean, and maybe this is going to cause a roadblock in your tunnel vision, the possibility does exist that the picture of a driver's license is something he pulled off a Google image search. Or maybe all these horny losers pass it around like the offering plate at church because they think they're too ugly to score a ten."

He checked Scarlet. "Correct me if I'm wrong, but I would imagine a guy who looks like Quasimodo isn't going to get a lot of play, even if he's got a jumbo-sized bankroll."

Scarlet looked from Jack to Carolina. "He's right about that much. I mean, some girls will see anyone who can pay, but the ones with a full roster... Looks definitely come into play."

Carolina felt this was all too far-fetched, but also saw how to spin it. "Then it's even more reason not to bring the cops in. If this is some random schlub and a dozen patrol cars show up with the cherries flashing and sirens crying, word's going to get out and any chance we had of being discrete is out the window."

She turned to her sister. "I'll take Max's Prius and you follow behind with Jack. As soon as you get eyes on the guy, you say whether it's the psycho or not. If it is, Jack you can call the cops and I'll detain the fucker until they get there."

She scanned the trio. "Sound like a plan?"

None of them looked overly confident, but no one protested out loud. She assumed that was as good as it was going to get.

CHAPTER FORTY

CAROLINA PULLED THE PRIUS TO THE SIDE OF THE ROAD, a few blocks from the hotel. Jack steered his sedan in behind her, parking it. She reached for pockets that weren't there, eager to pop a few pills before stepping out. Then she realized she had left them in the van.

She slammed her fist into the steering wheel, she'd have to deal with it later, and hoped her nerves would calm the old fashioned way.

She stepped out of her car, wrapped in a long, black trench coat that caught the wind as she walked.

She leaned into the window that Jack had rolled down.

"How much for an hour, doll?" Jack joked.

Carolina didn't laugh. "Funny guy."

She checked Scarlet in the passenger seat. All things considered she looked stable but anxious. "You okay?"

Scarlet shrugged. "Oh yeah. This is all normal."

"I'll head up to the hotel. Give me at least five minutes. If we go in together, it'll look suspicious."

"Agreed," Jack said. "But what happens if there's no time to assess the situation? After all, he's there to grab you and bag you, not wine and dine."

She pulled a stun gun from her pocket. "I've got this ready." She opened the small leather purse, something she never carried in real life, and revealed her pistol. "And this. A girl can't be too prepared."

"Good. But please don't stroll up and execute the guy. I don't have enough chits to call in to for that," Jack said.

Carolina smirked, but nervously. "I'll text you as soon as the guy makes contact with me."

Scarlet held up a pair of binoculars larger than her head. "And I came prepared. Just make sure he either steps out of the room or I have a clear view through the doorway."

"I will. I'll keep him busy with some talk, give you a good look. If it's not the guy, text me something, anything to get my phone buzzing. If I don't hear from you, I'll go inside and first chance I get I'll zap the bastard."

But she had no intention of doing that. She was going inside, closing the door, and blowing the fucker's head off. She'd say he attacked her and that she had no choice. Even though she doubted that story would fly when the cops arrived, she was prepared to accept the consequences.

"I'll text you as soon as he's incapacitated," Carolina said.

"And if you have any trouble, you scream your ever-loving head off," Jack said, his voice strong and affirming. "I'll kick down the door if need be." He gave her forearm a reassuring pat. "I'm not going to let anything bad happen to you. You've got my word."

She tried a smile, knowing he was doing his best to help. The guilt over lying to him was beginning to gnaw at her and she had to extricate herself from the conversation pronto.

"Great," she said. "I'll be in touch."

Jack nodded and she returned to the Prius, driving it the

last few blocks to the hotel. Her heart pounded, knowing she was only moments from seeing the monster face to face.

She parked in the front row where the cars aligned with the rooms, took out her cell, and messaged the killer.

In the parking lot.

Then she waited. A minute passed. Two. Five. Headlights swept across the lot as Jack's sedan entered.

You're too soon, she thought. You'll spook him.

But then her phone buzzed.

Great! I'm in 117. Can't wait!

Carolina took a deep breath. Exhaled. Took another. Then she opened the door and stepped into the night.

Room 117 was at the opposite end of the lot, far from the lobby. She counted the numbers on the doors and found it. The curtains were closed but light seeped around the edges.

She walked quickly, but carefully. Scarlet had wanted to give her stilettos, but Carolina refused and they compromised on two-inch heels. It was still more than Carolina was used to and the last thing she wanted was to take a swan dive in the parking lot before the action kicked off.

She passed 110. 111.

Her right hand fell to the purse, made sure it was unsnapped, fingered the cold metal of the gun. It would heat up soon enough.

What she wouldn't give for some pills right about now. She kicked herself for being in such a rush and leaving it behind. But she would be fine. Once she took this fucker down, she could overdose if she so desired. She needed a few more moments of steady nerves.

One last hard, dry swallow and she raised her left hand, knocking on the door to room 117.

CHAPTER FORTY-ONE

Jack didn't like the plan at all, but he'd always been helpless around beautiful women and around these two he had as much backbone as a lump of fresh putty.

He tried to convince himself what they said made sense, and it did in a way. The police weren't going to waste man hours investigating some missing hookers, not when there were revenue-generating ways to spend time, like writing traffic and parking tickets. Not when they could make headlines by taking down some cracker cooking meth in his public housing apartment. Not when the fine citizens of Pittsburgh put as much value on the lives of hookers as they did used gum wrappers in the gutter. As far as most folks were concerned, a dead hooker was a net positive to society.

The women had a point, but that didn't mean he enjoyed sitting next to a rape victim, trying to hunt down a serial killer, without a lifeline. Of all the mistakes he'd made in his career, this could be the stupidest one yet. And that was saying something.

He chuckled.

"What's funny?" Scarlet asked, her voice timid.

He had forgotten she was there for a moment. Her trauma. Her near death. And now her sister was in the line of fire.

And he was laughing. What a schmuck.

He cleared his throat. "I'm sorry, I just got lost in thought." He saw her staring with narrowed, suspicious eyes. "I was assessing the situation I currently find myself in. I never thought I'd be using my vacation time on something that might get me fired. Makes me question my sanity."

Scarlet nodded, and actually smiled. "Don't feel bad. My sister has a way of doing that to people."

She was still the damaged girl in his car, nervous and frightened. But her strength shocked him, as did her subsequent laugh.

He checked his watch. It seemed like they'd been sitting there for a quarter of an hour but it was only a few minutes. Nonetheless he put the car in gear and drove to the hotel that waited on the hill.

His eyes immediately went to the Prius and he saw Carolina's silhouette still inside it. That was good. He parked away from her, near a back corner and under an arc sodium flood light. He had no desire to sit in the dark.

Jack scanned the parking lot, making mental notes of all the vehicles. He tried to decide which one could belong to a killer. Maybe the late model Dodge pickup. Or perhaps the Ford Taurus with Bondo lining the rear wheel wells.

He considered inviting Scarlet to join him in this game, to pass the time and keep their minds occupied, but then the door to the Prius opened and Carolina climbed out.

"And here we go..." Jack said. She hadn't texted, as promised, but he decided to give a pass. Only one though.

She crossed the lot slowly and it seemed his own pulse

quickened with each step she took. Soon enough he could hear it firing in his ears.

Then she stopped at a door, took a quick pause, and knocked.

"You got that glass ready?" He looked to Scarlet and saw she already had the binoculars raised and was peering through them.

It was only three seconds, but they were the longest three seconds of Jack's life.

He watched Carolina raise her hand. He thought she was going to knock again, but instead she grabbed the knob, twisted it, and pushed the door inward.

No one stood there to greet her.

A breath caught in Jack's throat. This wasn't right. He reached for his door handle but Scarlet's voice stopped him.

"Wait," she said.

And, despite all his instincts, he did.

Then, Carolina stepped into the room and closed the door behind herself.

"What the holy hell does she think she's doing?" The words came out through clenched teeth. "This isn't the goddamn plan! We didn't even see the prick!"

"Jack, she knows what she's doing," Scarlet said. "She's trained for this."

He snapped his head toward her. "Did you two plan this behind my back? Am I just some rube you pulled in to clean up whatever mess is left behind?"

Scarlet lowered the binoculars. "We didn't. And you're not."

"Then explain to me what's going on."

Instead of an answer, he got a gunshot.

Jack and Scarlet sprinted to room 117. He was fully prepared to kick down the door—at least he could keep his promises—but it was unlocked.

They burst inside, expecting to find a dead body. Whose, he was not yet sure.

Only there was no body. There was no Carolina. No john.

He spotted a bullet hole in a pressboard bureau, then saw her pistol on the carpet. He looked past it and found Carolina's purse on the tile floor that separated the sink and makeup counter from the bathroom. The door to that room was closed.

He drew his gun, steeling himself, then thrust the door inward. The frame splintered as the door flew open, slamming against the bathroom wall. Chunks of cheap subway tile exploded upon impact, flying through the air like hailstones.

But the bathroom was empty too.

Jack jerked the shower curtain aside, ripping the vinyl free of rusted metal rings. The act revealed no people. What it showed was an open window.

Cool, evening air drifted inside and what happened was clear enough.

"Jack?" Scarlet's voice called from the main room.

He hurried out of the bathroom and saw her holding Carolina's cell and her stun gun. But he had no time for that. "Out back!"

Jack dashed past her, into the parking lot. He ran north, to the nearest end of the long building, cornered it, then kept running.

He was almost to the next corner when he heard tires tearing across the asphalt. Using every bit of stamina he had he quickened his pace, pistoning his feet.

He made the corner.

Just in time to see taillights exiting the lot. He strained to make out the vehicle, to hone in on any detail that he could use, but it was a generic, white SUV. The same type you see by the dozen parked at any mall or grocery store.

The son of a bitch was gone. And so was Carolina.

CHAPTER FORTY-TWO

Max took a swig of IC Light, relieved not to be part of the posse bringing down the killer. The last time he attempted to help Carolina under similar circumstances, he ended up shot, in need of two units of blood, and eight stitches. He was much better off as a consultant, or someone working behind the scenes. Being in the line of duty was not for him.

Besides, he could drink beer while he worked. Though *work* wasn't quite the right word for it. It was more like *worry*.

He regretted agreeing to Carolina's plan. He thought it needlessly risky and couldn't understand her desire to pull some Lone Ranger act when a couple phone calls would have the whole cavalry backing her up.

Her constant need to put her life in danger seemed almost suicidal and a part of him wondered if she was. Maybe that's why she popped painkillers like candy. And why she kept ending up in situations like this.

But this time might be better. Maybe it would all go as planned and she could play hero yet again. Only time would tell.

He just needed to be patient as no amount of worrying would change a damn thing. It probably helped that he was three beers in.

Just as he tried to relax, the door to Scarlet's apartment swung open. He was so startled the bottle tumbled from his hand and a long stream of yellow doused him from chest to groin, soaking Scarlet's couch in the process. Shit, he hoped she didn't make him pay for it. It would probably cost him a year's earnings.

"Fly in much?" Max asked, standing so fast he felt woozy. Maybe he'd overindulged.

He saw Jack and Scarlet, but no Carolina. He blinked, thinking he could be so drunk that he missed her, and took another look. Jack. Scarlet. No Carolina. Before he could ask—

"Carolina's gone," Jack said.

"Gone? What do you mean she's gone?" Max asked.

"It's four letters. What do you think I mean? The bastard took her by surprise or something. Must have knocked her out and took off through a rear window."

"Why didn't you stop him?" Max asked, still drunk, but fear was clearing his head. "That's why you were there, man!"

Jack marched to him, pressing his chest into Max's, their faces inches apart. "You think I don't know that, asshole!" He gave Max a hard shove but the couch broke his fall. "She's the one who deviated from the plan. She was supposed to bring him to the door, instead she walked right in. This is bullshit!"

Max bent at the waist, rubbing his temples, trying to get his thoughts straight. "I knew this whole idea was fucked."

"You're preaching to the choir," Jack said. "I never should have listened—"

"Hey!" Scarlet shouted, stealing their attention. "Stop trying to make yourselves feel superior and let's figure out how to get Carolina back."

She had a point.

"I'm calling the police," Max said, reaching for his phone.

"No!" Jack ordered.

"Come on, man. Carolina was a cop. They'll get involved now."

"No way, we can't call the cops," Jack said.

"Why not?" Max yelled.

"Because Carolina didn't want them involved," Jack said.

This was ridiculous logic as far as Max was concerned. "I don't think she gets a vote anymore."

"But I do," Scarlet said.

Max stared at her. Surely she had to be on his side. "And what do you say?"

Scarlet gave both the men a long, hard look. "I say no police. They didn't give a fuck about me or Eve or the girl he brought in the night I escaped. And we don't have any new information to give them anyway. All they'll do is detain us and question us for who the hell knows how long. And that's time that we can't afford to lose. Because while they're holding us, that fucker has Carolina and he'll be..."

She couldn't finish the sentence, but everyone knew what would happen once he had Carolina in his barn.

And she had a point. In this situation, every minute mattered.

"Well, shit," Max said. "Then what's the new plan? Because the old one just shit the bed."

"What about the address?" Scarlet asked.

"I told you before, none of those lead to a farm. Or anything close."

Jack's head snapped to attention. "What address? What are you talking about?"

"There was a partial on the driver's license pic. Nineteen fifty-three Sequoia something. But I already searched it. There are like eight dozen within a hundred miles and they're all—"

A vein in Jack's temple looked on the verge of blowing and his face flared red. "Why am I just hearing about this now?"

Max pivoted his eyes to Scarlet, she did the same. Both looked like school kids trying to hide wrongdoing from the principal.

"I, uh, thought Carolina told you," Max mumbled, feeling two inches tall.

"Fucking hell!" Jack yelled. "You morons drag me into this because you want me to cover your ass, but then you withhold something like that? I ought to arrest you for being goddamned idiots!"

Jack spun away from them, fists clenched, pacing at warp speed. Max could practically see him counting from one to ten in his head, trying to calm down. He knew he should keep his mouth shut, but timing had never been his strong suit.

"Dude," Max said. "We already tried running with this and it didn't go anywhere."

Jack leaned into the kitchen island folding his hands together. "Oh, you ran with it?"

Max nodded. Scarlet too.

"So, I take that to mean you visited each of those addresses. Questioned the people who lived there. You know, the boring shit law enforcement does on the daily?"

He didn't wait for a response. "Of course you didn't, because you're not fucking cops! You're a hooker and a hack teamed up with a thirty-year-old Nancy Drew wannabe and I don't think any of the three of you could recognize the difference between your own assholes and holes in the ground! Instead of using the one real piece of evidence you have, you decided the best option is going undercover and running your own personal sting."

Jack stomped away from them, heading toward the bathroom. "Print out that list of addresses. I don't care if there are five hundred. As soon as it's a reasonable hour, when people are out of their beds, we start knocking on doors."

Jack disappeared into the bathroom, locking the door behind him.

Max turned to Scarlet. "I think that was a little harsh."

All she could do was nod.

CHAPTER FORTY-THREE

Carolina's head throbbed. Her thoughts came slow and clumsy. She had no clue what was going on or where she was.

She laid prone on her back. Everything hurt. Old injuries. New. Her body was a fireball of pain as every nerve seemed to be misfiring in unison.

Pushing through the misery, she rolled onto her side to work her way into a sitting position. When she did that, she felt hard, needle-like straw poke into the exposed skin of her arms, legs, and face.

Her eyes fluttered, opened, but she didn't need sight to know where she was.

The barn.

She noticed the metal cuff on her ankle and allowed her head to fall backward, clunking against the barn wall. That sent a clap of pain thundering through her skull and she reached to examine the spot with her fingers. A wet, sticky wound seeped blood, turning her newly bleached locks strawberry blonde.

You fucked up this time, she thought. *A fuckup of epic proportions.*

She remained clad in Scarlet's red dress and did a quick underwear check. Still there, thank God. At least the bastard hadn't raped her while she was out.

Small victory.

Especially since that part would come soon enough. Unless she could find a way out.

Carolina checked the wall remembering that Scarlet had broken the wood that held the chain. Maybe she could do the same.

But now a fresh two by six was screwed into the wall, and thick bolts held the chain fast. She gave it a tug but already knew it wasn't budging.

Now what?

A sniffle caught Carolina's attention. Her eyes drifted from her own confinement, to the stall across from her own prison. There she found a battered woman around the same age as Scarlet.

Blonde, of course, and she'd been wearing a nice dress once upon a time but now it was rags. From how Scarlet had described her, Carolina was sure this was the girl who'd been brought in the night of her escape.

At least she was still alive. There was that much.

Another small victory.

Carolina had a feeling she was going to need all of those she could get.

"What's your name?" she asked the girl.

"Laurie," she whispered. "I wasn't sure you were alive." She crept forward in her stall, coming closer. "You've just been laying there for hours."

"Not dead yet." Carolina moved as far toward the girl as her chain would allow. At the end of their restraints, six feet still separated them. "I don't remember much of how I got here, though."

"He carried you in, slung over his shoulder like you were light as a feather."

Carolina had assumed that much. What she meant was how she got from the hotel to the farm. She remembered opening the door to the hotel room. Hearing a voice. 'In the bathroom washing up. Come in,' it had said. And she obeyed.

She'd drawn her pistol and didn't plan on asking any questions. Stepping toward the bathroom, ready to shoot, she was hit from behind. She recalled pulling the trigger as she went down, but after that her mind went blank.

Jack must be so pissed at me, she thought. She hoped he'd get a chance to berate her in person. But the odds seemed slim.

She breathed a few short, shallow breaths, felt ready to climb out of her own skin. Some of it was panic, but she also knew she was going into withdrawal. As if this could get any fucking worse.

"Calm down," Laurie said. Like it was that easy.

"We need to find a way out," Carolina said, also stating the obvious.

The girl let out a tired, defeated laugh. One snort of air. "No chance," she said. "I've been trying for days."

"There's a chance. I know because my sister got away. If she can, so can we."

"Your sister? The girl who took off the night he got me? She's your sister?"

Carolina nodded. "I used to be a cop. She told me about him and we were trying to set him up so we could find this place and you."

"I kept hoping she'd send help back, but after so long..." Laurie began to sob. "Oh, praise Jesus."

"Don't get ahead of yourself," Carolina said. "Nobody knows where we are."

"What? You just said—"

The barn door swung open and a male figure appeared, back lit by the orange light of dawn. Laurie crab-crawled backward in her stall, curling into a tight ball. But Carolina held her ground and watched him come.

He was just like Scarlet had described, but his smell was still a shock. It preceded him as he moved into the barn, a cross between shit and yeast and world record B.O.

He was average in stature, possibly on the small side. He pushed some of the matted hair out of his eyes and she saw his feral, rodent-like face.

It was worse than she'd imagined.

"You up," he said, pointing at her. "I'm glad."

She noticed he held an oblong box in his hands and, as he came closer to her, he extended it to her.

"What is that?" she asked.

"A game. I want to play," he said.

"P-Play?" she asked, wondering if play was codeword for rape.

He nodded, giving an *mmm hmm* along with it. He sat cross-legged in front of her.

So many thoughts ran wild in her head about what he was going to do with her. To her. Whether the others could pull off some miracle and pin down this location. Or how she could find a way out on her own. Because that's what it always came down to. Doing it on her own.

Her fingers toyed with the chain and she wondered if she could slowly work her way back into the stall, creating enough slack with which to strangle him. Before she could even begin, he opened the box.

She'd expected something gruesome, maybe a collection of fingers, a dead rodent, or a weapon. Instead, it was Jenga. She almost laughed.

"I like this game. It's hard," he said.

"I like it too," Carolina said, trying to keep him on her side for as long as possible. "What's your name?"

He paused, looking up from the tower of blocks. "Not supposed to say."

"It's okay. You can tell me. I'm Carolina," she said before she could stop and remind herself that, to him, she was Jezebel. The man either didn't notice or ignored it. "Now that you know my name, you can tell me yours."

He bit into his lower lip with crooked, rotting teeth. Finally, he spoke. "Earl." But he looked away from her when he said it, back to the game. "You go first."

She nodded and reached out. "Okay." Her hand trembled and she realized that her opioid consumption was more than just a little problem. This was bound to be a short game. She extracted one piece, then set it aside.

"My turn!" Earl shouted.

At his exclamation, Laurie's crying increased in volume. "Where are they?" she screamed. "When are they coming?"

Carolina wanted to tell her to shut up, but she also didn't want to tip the man that anything was amiss.

"Be quiet!" he commanded.

"I'm sorry," Laurie bawled. Her crying didn't stop though.

As Earl went to grab a block, the girl unleashed a wracking sob. He almost knocked over the tower, steadying himself at the last second.

"You ruin all the fun!" He jumped to his feet, left Carolina's stall, and grabbed a grain shovel.

Before either of the women could react, he reared back with the shovel, then swung it down in the girl's head. She slumped backward, collapsing sideways onto the dirt floor. Blood drained down her face in crimson rivulets.

With her quiet, Earl left the stall, set the shovel aside, and returned to Carolina. He sat down, a wretched grin tugging at his mouth. "Your turn!"

CHAPTER FORTY-FOUR

THEY WERE ON THE ROAD BEFORE DAWN BROKE AND AT the first Sequoia property by seven a.m. That was a bust, as were the next fourteen properties they tried. Those were the closest, the ones in the outlying suburbs. Now they were hitting towns half an hour from the city and further and after another thirty or so, there was still no luck.

Why couldn't the address have been something more unique, Jack thought. He'd grown up on Wysocki Avenue and he'd bet his left nut there weren't a hundred of those in Western Pennsylvania. But he supposed it could have been worse. It could have been Elm Street.

It was almost three in the afternoon as they rolled into yet another 1953 Sequoia property. This one was nearly an hour southeast, in Westmoreland County. The house was a squat, one-story brick ranch with a sensible Kia Sportage parked in the driveway.

Jack was growing weary of the constant failure and for the first time in months he seriously considered breaking into the pack of emergency cigarettes he kept in his briefcase.

He said a quick prayer to the big man upstairs, trying to cut a deal. *Let this be the place and I won't go back to sucking on those coffin nails. What do you say, God?*

If they didn't stumble across something worthwhile soon, he would be forced to call this in and then there would be hell to pay.

Fouling up that investigation in Buffalo had been one thing, but it was an honest mistake. Running this shit show of an undercover op, off the books, with a victim's family and some hack blogger, going rogue, using his badge without official Agency clearance...

He'd be lucky to emerge from this mess with his pension. Hell, he might end up doing time himself. This is what he got for being a nice guy.

He heard Max open one of the sedan's rear doors and watched him via the rearview mirror. Scarlet occupied the passenger seat, but she'd been withdrawn and quiet, crying when she thought neither of the men would notice.

Up until this point, Max had been the Hardy to his Laurel and he enjoyed working with the kid. He was quick-witted and read people well. But that act worked when they were in the city, or at least adjacent to it. Now they were in the sticks where some people still wore their prejudice like a well-earned merit badge.

"Maybe hold up there, chief," Jack said to Max.

Max looked at his eyes in the mirror. "Why?"

"I just think it's better if I handle this one."

Max raised his eyebrows, curious. "Same question, man. Why?"

Jack took in the neighborhood, so typical of rural, small town America. And even though they were north of the Mason Dixon more than a few Confederate flags swayed in the morning air.

"Don't take this the wrong way, but you're a little... darker, than these kinds of folks are used to having showing up on their doorsteps."

"Oh, hell no," Max said. "You didn't go there."

"Hey, I don't like it either," Jack said. "But we need cooperation. So just placate me, okay?"

Max slumped back in the seat, arms crossed tight over his chest. Jack was content to let him pout.

He exited the vehicle, traversing a narrow brick walkway through which grass and weeds had sprouted. Another season and it would be lost to nature. The whole place had a neglected look to it. The windows were streaked and in need of washing. The gutters overflowed with fallen leaves. The mailbox hanging beside the entrance had a broken door that hung askew. Whoever lived here wasn't keen on routine maintenance.

Jack rapped on the door. Three firm knocks. He waited fifteen seconds and added three more.

With no response he was ready to give up not just on this house, but life in general. He was halfway back to his rental when he heard a deadbolt snap and the door open.

"Sir?" a woman's voice that sounded as dry as a creek bed in August, called out.

Jack turned back expecting to find a shriveled up prune of a human being, but who he saw didn't quite fit that mold. She was older, but not ancient. Late-sixties, maybe even a little younger, but her lead gray hair added some miles. She wore a floral print housecoat and slippers that looked like cats.

"Can I help you?" she asked.

He returned to her, keeping a professional distance as he put on his most charming smile. "I'm sorry to bother you, ma'am. I'm Special Agent Jack Burrell with the FBI and I'm working on a missing person's case."

Her pale, hazel eyes grew wide. "Are you talking about Reginald?"

Jack took a step closer. "Reginald?"

She nodded. "My husband."

"Can I show you something?" Jack asked.

She nodded and he pulled the print out of the john's driver's license. It had been folded and unfolded so many times the ink was beginning to wear off at the creases.

"This man is a person of interest." He turned the photo her way.

She took it in with patient, knowing eyes. "Yes that's Reggie. Have you found him?"

Jack wondered if he'd misheard her. If his mind was so desperate for a hit that it was tricking his ears.

"The man in the driver's license photo is your husband?" he asked.

"Yes, that's what I said. Now can you please explain what's going on? Is something wrong with Reggie? Did something happen to him?"

Jack gulped in a mouthful of air and his eyes darted skyway. Thanks, big guy.

"Is it alright if I come in so we can talk?"

The woman nodded.

HER NAME WAS Virginia Ripken and she insisted on fetching Jack a cup of coffee—no cream or sugar please—before they delved into why he was there. When she returned with their drinks, he was sitting on a microfiber loveseat, browsing through her Reader's Digest.

"Here you are." She handed over one cup and kept the other for herself. Then she sat in a worn recliner, propping her feet, still sheathed in cat slippers, on an equally tired futon.

She took another look at the photo of her husband. "Reggie always hated that picture. Said it made his face look fat. I tried to tell him it's just for identification, not a glamour shot."

Virginia Ripken passed the photo back to Jack who refolded and returned it to his pocket.

"It seems like we're coming into this from two different directions," Jack said. "You asked if I found your husband. Is he missing?"

The woman sipped her coffee. "I don't exactly know, Mr.... What did you say your name was again?"

"Burrell."

She gave a quick nod. "Mr. Burrell. I haven't seen Reggie for nearly six months, but I also haven't seen his clothing, his car, his most prized possessions like that damnable baseball card collection. And I certainly haven't seen any of his money either."

It began to make more sense. "He left you?"

Another sip of coffee. "After forty-four years of marriage I didn't get so much as a, 'Goodbye and thanks for the memories,' from him. I'd been out of town, visiting our son for a few days and when I returned home, Reggie was gone, along with his belongings and our bank account. Left me with nothing but bills and a broken heart."

"I'm very sorry to hear that," Jack said. "Do you have any idea where he might have gone?"

"No sir. If I did I'd have tracked him down myself for nothing other than the pleasure of shoving my foot up his ass."

That made him smile. The old girl had some moxie. "With the slippers or without?" he asked.

"With." She smirked. "If I had to guess, I'd say he took off with one of his trollops."

"He had a mistress?" Jack asked.

"Multitudes. I tolerated it because that's what women of my generation do, but I wasn't half the fool he took me for." She went for another drink of tea but seemed to lose herself in thought. "Although, considering where I am now, maybe I was."

"Don't let a man's bad habits define you," Jack said, trying to reassure her. He also wanted to get the conversation back on track.

"Does he have any family, brothers or sisters, whom he may have kept in contact with?"

"He had an older brother, Warren, but he passed some years back."

"You mentioned having a son. Has he heard from your husband?"

"Not a word. But Reggie was never close to him. Our son has... special needs. I think Reggie was ashamed of that. He was a very successful man, ran his own business for over three decades. I don't think he could ever accept having a son who was incapable of filling his shoes."

"Is your son in a group home, or an institution?"

Virginia brightened. "Oh no. It's not to that extreme. He lives on my family's homestead. Works the farm that's been ours for four generations."

Her voice was proud, but Jack could only hone in on one word.

Farm.

"And where is this farm?" Please be in the state, he thought. This has to be it.

"About an hour to the east. Just outside of Somerset."

Bingo. We've got you now, you sleazy son of a bitch. But Jack was careful not to let his glee show. "Could you give me the address? I might head over that way."

"Oh, you're welcome to, but Earl hasn't heard from Reggie since he left us. He'd tell me if he did. He knows how hard it's been on me since his father ran off."

"I understand. It's just procedure. You know, crossing t's, dotting i's."

Virginia smiled and nodded. "Of course. The farm's located on a rural route though, nothing you can put in your phone or GPS. But I'd be happy to show you the way. I have no plans and it's a nice day for a drive."

"I really hate to put you out."

Virginia was already standing. "Nonsense. Just let me put on some real clothes and I'll meet you outside."

CHAPTER FORTY-FIVE

Carolina and Earl played four games of Jenga and in none of them did she manage to remove more than four blocks before sending the whole thing crashing down. The first time, Earl laughed. The second he grinned. But, after the last two failures, whatever patience he possessed reached its limits.

He slammed his fist into the fallen tower, sending chunks of wood flying across the floor. "You don't even try!" he screamed in her face, then stomped out of the barn and she hadn't seen him since.

Only, Carolina was trying. The harder she tried, the more she shook. It wasn't just her hands either. Her whole body felt like she was sitting on a vibrating bed. The sweats kicked in too, saturating her dress, and in the cool, fall air she felt on the verge of hypothermia.

Between withdrawal and Earl's stench lingering in the barn, she fought not to vomit. She could feel the previous day's food roiling in her stomach. It wouldn't stay down much longer.

The culmination of all of it hit her like an avalanche. And she'd only been there hours. How did Scarlet tolerate this day after day after day? Carolina knew she'd lose her mind if this went on too long.

Meanwhile, Laurie hadn't moved since Earl bashed her with the shovel. Carolina tried to focus, to see if her chest rose and fell. But, as far as her bleary eyes could see, there was no activity.

"Laurie!" Carolina half-whispered, half-hissed. "Laurie, are you okay?"

No response.

She risked raising her voice into a near shout. "Laurie!"

As the sound of her voice died off, the barn door slid open, grinding on its track. Earl's shadow spilled inside, stretching ahead of him like a ghostly specter. He stomped toward the women, his booted feet sending up plumes of dust. This time, he carried no game.

"Why are you talking to her?" he asked, his voice booming.

"I—I was making sure she was okay," Carolina said.

Earl's upper lip pulled back in a sneer. He grabbed onto Carolina's right arm and slung her like a discus. As she spun, her feet got tangled up in the chain and she lost her balance, slamming into the stall wall. The back of her arm caught on an exposed nail, ripping open her flesh and blood so hot it felt boiling drained from the wound.

"You talk to me. No one else!" Earl ordered.

"Okay," Carolina said. "No one but you, Earl. I promise." But her eyes went back to Laurie's motionless figure. "It's just, you hit her really hard earlier. She might need help."

Earl turned toward Laurie and he trudged into her stall. He grabbed a fistful of her hair, raising her face out of the dirt, then slapped her across the mouth. Still, she didn't move.

"She's boring. No fun anymore." He dropped her and her limp body landed with a dull thud.

"You should be nicer to her," Carolina said. "Then, she could play."

"Daddy always said bad kids need a whoopin' when they don't behave. Daddy said a whooping is good for the soul." His shoulders heaved as he breathed hard.

If Carolina didn't do something fast, he'd finish the woman off. If she wasn't already gone. Maybe he'd stomp her skull in with his boots. Maybe he'd wring her neck with his powerful, calloused hands. Or maybe he'd grab some other tool and use it on her. Either way, she felt like she must intervene.

"Well, I'm good though, right, Earl? You won't ever have to whoop on me, right?"

He turned his attention to Carolina and away from the girl, which was somehow a relief. Then he moved to her, crouching in a catcher's stance before her. It put his eyes at the perfect angle to peer down her dress, to ogle her cleavage.

Earl licked his lips, tongue dragging across his jagged, misaligned teeth. "I ain't gonna whoop you," he said. "Not now. Now, we're gonna play my favorite game."

He stood, unbuckled his belt, unsnapped his jeans.

Carolina hopped to her feet and scurried backward, not stopping until she hit the wall. Her spine collided with the bolts locking down her chain, sending electric shocks coursing through her back.

In her life, hell, in the last few weeks, she'd endured so much. But she wasn't going to let this monster inside her. She'd stop him, or die trying.

"Earl, I can't play that game right now. I need food first. Aren't you going to feed me?"

"Not now," he said. "Later. I'm always hungry after playing. When we done, I'll make you a sandwich. Oscar Mayer bologna." Then he spelled the last word in a singsong voice. "B O L O G N A."

Earl shook his narrow hips and his jeans dropped to the floor. He wore no underwear, giving her a too good look at his manhood. He might be small in stature but he wasn't between the legs.

His uncircumcised cock, still limp and stained with dried blood and his own putrid excrement, dangled between his legs like a black snake. His oversized scrotum swung, a clock pendulum counting down the moments before her misery.

"Take off your clothes," he ordered.

"Just get me a drink first. Please," she said, but she had little hope left at this point. "Some water. You haven't given me anything to drink since I got here, remember. You have to take care of me, just like you do the pigs, if you want me to be able to play."

Earl's only response was a grunt. He pulled his jeans over his boots, then moved toward her, halving the distance between them.

Carolina's gaze darted around the stall, looking for something, anything she could use as a weapon. But there was nothing. She was alone and helpless. She was at his mercy and he had none.

Why couldn't I at least be high, she thought, yearning for pills that could numb what was to come. She'd lived so much of the last year in that fog, why did she now have to be clear-headed. It was like a sick, cosmic joke at her expense.

Or maybe it was her penance.

Earl was closer, two yards away. She saw old blood on his groin, smeared on his thighs, across his belly. She knew some of that blood was Scarlet's. Some was Laurie's. Some was Eve's.

And soon, some will be mine, she thought.

All the nausea she'd been fighting off since regaining consciousness hit. The levy she'd constructed inside herself broke, and her stomach contents exploded from her mouth.

Her partially digested stomach contents hit Earl, projectile style, battering his chest and stomach, some splashing onto his face, landing in his mouth. She felt like a low rent Linda Blair, but it bought her a distraction.

Earl jumped backward, his arms windmilling as he tried to wipe her puke away. He made childish *Awk Ack* sounds that leaked out between his own gags. He spit and coughed and still kept trying to cleanse himself of Carolina's vomit.

This was her best—her only—chance and she knew it. Earl stood, feet spread apart, completely ignoring her in his disgusted panic. And Carolina knew what to do.

She sprinted at him and funneled every bit of strength she possessed into her untethered leg. Earl saw her at the last second, as her foot was already coming up, but he was too slow or her foot was moving too fast, or both.

Either way he was helpless to stop what was coming.

Carolina's foot landed square and landed hard. She felt it sink into the soft tissue between Earl's legs. Felt a splash of hot wetness that made her think he pissed himself, then all her thoughts were drowned out by his screams.

Earl stumbled backward, howling in agony. His hands had forgotten about the vomit and went to his crotch. So did Carolina's gaze.

Even she couldn't have expected what she found. Earl's scrotum had ruptured under the impact wrought by her foot and the flesh of his sack hung in loose, hairy tendrils. What looked like rotten cottage cheese mixed with blood and semi-coagulated fat spilled from that broken mass and his two testicles dangled in the breeze, held only by random veins and tubes.

The sounds coming from his mouth were inhuman, an exquisite symphony of misery to her listening ears. Carolina considered rushing him, grabbing hold of those exposed balls, and tearing them free. He deserved that. And more. But Earl's retreat continued and he was out of reach.

With something like a combination of a bellow, yodel, and

howl he stumbled away, out of the barn disappearing into the barnyard.

"Take that, motherfucker," she said, unable to remove the smile from her face. "You might kill me, but you won't rape me."

That had worked far better than Carolina could have ever hoped, but she knew it only bought her some time. He'd be back. Or maybe he'd bleed out and die. Either way she was still chained to the wall. A prisoner.

She had to find a way to free herself.

CHAPTER FORTY-SIX

"I really feel like I should have a gun," Max said.

"Same," Scarlet said.

Jack stole glances at them as he followed the Kia up the long, dirt driveway. "Do either of you even know how to use a firearm?" Jack asked.

"I was money at Duck Hunt," Max said.

Scarlet didn't say anything.

"That's about what I thought," Jack said.

He'd shared what he learned from Virginia, the missing husband, the son with the farm, as they drove. The pieces went together easy enough in theory.

The son could have obtained his father's driver's license. Maybe he stole it, or maybe something more nefarious occurred. Either way, Reginald Ripken wasn't what any of them cared about. All that mattered, at this point, was finding Carolina.

The brake lights on the Kia illuminated and it slowed to a stop. Ahead stood a hundred-year-old farmhouse. Beyond that, at least a football field length away, a barn.

The Sportage's door opened and Virginia climbed out. Jack and the others followed suit.

"I don't see any vehicles," Jack said. "Do you think your son's home?"

Virginia nodded. "He usually parks his pickup behind the barn. He doesn't go anywhere except the feed mill and butcher shop. Earl's a homebody."

Jack liked the woman and hated keeping his suspicions from her, but thought it better she remain carefree, unaware of the monster she'd birthed.

"Virginia, why don't you check out the animals, see if Earl's tending to them. I'll head up to the house."

"Alright," she said. "Oh." She held up the keys. "The house is usually unlocked, but just in case. The gold key's the one to the front door." She passed them to Jack.

As the woman strolled toward the pasture, Jack turned his attention to Scarlet.

"Any of this look familiar?" he asked.

Her eyes scanned the grounds. He could tell she was straining to find a reason to say yes, but she ended up shaking her head. "I don't know. It was dark and all I really cared about was running. The house looks like it might be the same, but I'd probably say that about any farmhouse. They all have that look, you know?"

"It's okay," Jack said. "I want you both to stay here, with the car. Have your phones dialed to nine one one. First sign anything is amiss, you call. Got it?"

He expected them to protest, but neither did.

Scarlet reached out, ran her fingers across his sleeve. "Be careful, Jack."

"I will," he said. "Careful's my middle name."

"I thought it was Shawn," Max said, with a smirk.

Jack shook his head. The kid was right. "This guy," he said. "Thinks he's so smart..."

With that, he left them.

As Virginia has suspected, the front door was unlocked. Jack dropped the keys into his jacket pocket, took out his pistol, and stepped inside.

"Earl?" he called. "Earl, are you in here?"

No response came and he continued into the house, finding nothing but one empty room after another.

"My name's Jack and I'm a Special Agent with the FBI. Your mother brought me here. I need to ask you a couple questions about your father."

More silence.

He peered up the stairway that led to the second floor, but decided to save that for last.

Just beyond the bottom landing stood the dining room. The long, oak table was covered in years' worth of dust, with the exception of a lone spot at the head of the table. That area had been wiped clean by elbows, plates, activity. Well, clean was subjective. Bits of spilled food littered the area, flies teeming over it, feasting and laying eggs simultaneously.

"Disgusting," Jack muttered to himself.

Lining the walls, there were a variety of trinkets. Collectable plates, ancient embroidery, a faded print of The Last Supper. A corner cabinet was almost overflowing with handmade dolls, the kind that Jack thought might come to life when you slept and cut your throat.

"Creepy shit..."

As he went deeper into the house, the amount of filth and disorganization grew exponentially. One room, probably a study or library judging by the bookshelves, was piled full of newspapers, boxes and cans of long expired food, and heaps of clothing. Some of the clothing belonged to women, and it wasn't the kind Virginia would have worn. Rodent droppings fouled all of it.

As he turned down a hallway, he saw blood on the floor. Large amounts of it. It was an obvious trail and Jack followed, moving his index finger from the trigger guard, to the trigger.

He moved slower than the typical sloth as the trail led him to a closed door. As he reached for the doorknob, he steeled himself. "Earl?" he called again. "Are you in there? I'm from the FBI. I'm here to help."

Jack knew no answer was coming, so he raised the gun and opened the door.

The act revealed the first floor bathroom where the linoleum was slick with gore. The carnage led to a completely nude, save for his boots, Earl, sitting on the edge of a clawfoot bathtub. He held a blood-soaked towel to his groin and only looked up when Jack inhaled sharply.

"Holy shit! What happen—"

Before he could finish the word, Earl dove at him. The collision sent Jack's pistol skittering away, out of reach amidst the plumbing.

The agent was on his back, Earl atop him. Jack felt hot blood from the man's crotch seep into his own clothes. He had a moment to be disgusted, another to think, *I should fight back*, but then Earl was lashing out at him. He held a pair of scissors and the blades sunk into Jack's forehead, flaying it open to the bone.

Earl swung again, that time in a stabbing motion. The blade sunk through Jack's cheek, shattering a molar. He sucked a mouthful of broken tooth into his airway coughing, hacking, trying to breathe.

But Earl was relentless. A cut to his shoulder. A stab in his stomach. A slash across his lips.

The next volley took out Jack's right eye. Any chance of

fending off the coming blows was gone, lost in a red haze with no depth perception.

Earl rammed the scissors into Jack's chest, a hard crack as they hit ribs. He reared back, swung again. That time the blades sunk into Jack's neck. When Earl ripped them free, Jack could breathe again.

But only for a second. Then he was choking—no—drowning in his own blood.

Earl's onslaught continued, but it mattered naught.

Jack Burrell was dead.

CHAPTER FORTY-SEVEN

Carolina knelt before the nail which had ripped her arm open, like she was praying to a statue of Christ on the cross. She tried to rock the nail back and forth enough to free it. The hope, the plan, was to use the nail to pick the lock holding the cuff to her leg. It seemed far-fetched, even to her, but it was all she had to work with.

If she couldn't pick the lock, she could always use the nail to slit her own throat. She was, after all, an optimist.

The skin on her fingertips was raw and bloody from the effort, the slickness making the act even more challenging. She considered using her teeth to pull when—

The hogs went wild in the pen behind her. Snorting, whining. The noise they made when Earl was coming. When they were about to get fed.

She'd assumed the destroyed ball sack would buy her more time, but it appeared as if her time was almost up. She pulled harder at the nail, desperate, frantic. Then, her hand slipped and the nail slid under her thumbnail which bent askew with a hard snap, splitting down the middle. She bit her tongue to stifle a scream.

The frantic calls of the hogs lessened. That meant Earl was passing them by, continuing on to the barn. To her.

"Earl?" a woman's voice called out. "Hon? You in here? There's a fellow, got some questions about Daddy."

Carolina crept forward in the stall, trying to remain hidden until she could see who was there. To assure herself this wasn't Earl putting on some sick falsetto to toy with her.

And then she saw her. A senior citizen type, her gray hair pulled back in a loose ponytail, face a roadmap of wrinkles. Virginia Ripken.

"Help me," Carolina cried, her voice cracking with emotion and exhaustion.

Virginia saw her, her eyes turning to saucers. "Oh my God," the woman gasped, rushing to her.

Carolina fell into her arms. "You have to get me out of here!"

"What happened to y—"

Carolina held up her chain. "This is bolted to the wall. Get a pry bar or an ax or something. Hurry!"

Virginia nodded, but seemed frozen in place. She'd spotted Laurie still unmoving in the straw. "Oh Lord," she said. "Oh Lord please, this can't be real. This can't be."

Carolina grabbed her by the shoulders, gave her a firm shake. "Listen. He'll be back. You have to help me."

Virginia nodded, her ponytail bouncing. "I will. I promise." With that she was gone, hurrying out of the barn.

Carolina stared at the open door, mumbling random pleas.

"Help," the woman yelled. "Someone, help! He's got girls in the ba—"

Crack!

The noise was so loud Carolina could feel it. And no other cries for help followed.

CHAPTER FORTY-EIGHT

"DID YOU HEAR THAT?" SCARLET ASKED.

Max had been staring into the bucolic landscape, pondering why cities got such a bad rap when shit like this happened in the heartland. "Hear what?"

"I don't know. A voice. Maybe Virginia."

Max cocked his head, straining to hear. "I got nothing."

Scarlet had been sitting against the hood of the Prius, a position that annoyed Max—he was still making payments, after all—but he hadn't said anything. "How long's Jack been in there?" she asked.

Max checked the time on his phone. "Not long. Six minutes."

"Feels longer."

He nodded. "Yeah. It does."

"Maybe we should go check," she suggested.

"He'll be pissed if we do."

Scarlet slid off the car, stepping toward the house. "So, let him be pissed."

Max started to follow when a gunshot echoed across the flatland.

A cloud of blackbirds exploded from a wheat field, their black forms dotting the otherwise pristine, blue October sky. As the gunshot faded out, it was replaced with the frantic, hungry sounds of pigs squealing.

All of that noise came from the barn, so that's where Max and Scarlet dashed.

CHAPTER FORTY-NINE

CAROLINA FLINCHED AT THE SOUND OF THE GUNSHOT. Then flinched again when the hogs went crazy.

That poor woman, she thought, killed by her own son. Though, perhaps a quick death would be preferable to living with her son's crimes hanging over her head. Either way, it added to the tragedy. And it meant Carolina's salvation had just been extinguished.

She'd be next, of course. It played out like a movie clip in front of Carolina's eyes. Earl would stumble inside, his balls still dripping, step up to her and end her.

Or maybe he'd torture her first. Shoot her in the groin as payback for what she'd done to his twig and berries. Then grab a knife and start cutting off pieces of her, feeding them to the pigs, while she watched.

The options were near endless and none of them were comely. Aware she'd never pry free the nail in time, she decided to use it in a different manner.

Carolina slammed her forearm into the nail, sinking it deep, then gave her arm a hard jerk. It ripped a seven-inch channel through her flesh, a wound that bled profusely.

Dropping onto her ass, she used the flowing blood to slick the cuff and grease her ankle. She made sure every visible inch was slathered, then started pulling.

The steel sliced into her calf. She pulled again, creating a new, deeper cut. Again, again, again. If she was going to get it out, she might need to deglove her entire foot in the process. And she was willing to go that far because Carolina finally decided she wanted to live.

More pulling, more bleeding. There was a gash all the way around her ankle now. The skin below it moved in unison, like it existed separate from the rest of her body. She gave another hard yank and that skin shimmied down her calf, bunching above her heel.

The mass of it was caught in the cuff, preventing it from moving further. She would have to peel that flesh from her foot as the cuff couldn't make the pivot from her calf to her foot otherwise.

Gritting her teeth she grabbed a handful of skin and began to pull it down, creating a pain that made getting shot in the shoulder feel like a bee sting. It was like her foot was on fire, soaking in acid, and being stabbed by a million knives all at once.

It was so intense her vision clouded and her head began to take on that lighter than air feeling that came just before you passed out. Keep your shit together, she told herself. This is no time to puss out.

And then footsteps came into the barn. They were awkward and staggering. Earl's footsteps as he tried to push through his own misery.

Carolina moved the heaped up skin another quarter inch. Then half. Just as she was closing in on a full inch of progress, she saw—

Virginia. The front of the woman's plain, blue blouse was soaked with blood.

Carolina's first thought was that she was bleeding out, but had managed to stumble back inside so she could apologize before dying.

Then Carolina saw the shotgun in Virginia's hand. She held it loosely by the grip, the barrel dragging through the straw as she moved to the stall.

"I just shot my boy. I just shot my boy," Virginia said over and over again, her face ghostly white with shock.

Carolina wanted to reach out to her, to embrace her, to thank her, but her foot was an anchor and all she could do was sit and stare.

"I shot Earl," Virginia said and the shotgun fell from her hands, clattering to the ground. "My God, what have I done?" She steadied herself against a beam. It was all that held her upright.

"You saved my life. That's what you've done. My life and maybe hers." She looked to Laurie who still appeared catatonic, at best.

Virginia pushed off the beam and moved to her, half crouching, half falling to her side. Carolina wrapped her arms around Virginia's shoulders as the woman wept. She didn't tell her that crying was for sissies. In fact, she joined her.

Then she saw a new shape at the barn door and tensed, as if Earl was a slasher movie villain who refused to die. But, it was Scarlet and Max. They ran toward Carolina, but she returned her attention to the woman who was the reason she was alive.

"Thank you," Carolina whispered in her ear. "Thank you."

CHAPTER FIFTY

A HODGEPODGE OF STATE AND LOCAL POLICE SWARMED THE farm. Carolina had a feeling the FBI would be there soon too, as soon as word of Jack Burrell's murder reached the right person.

She felt the worst about him. If she hadn't dragged him into this mess he'd probably be running stolen credit card numbers or packing his bags for that vacation in Boca. Something simple and safe. Instead he was in a body bag being wheeled to a waiting hearse. It would take a long time to forgive herself.

Before the police arrived Carolina had considered making up some elaborate lie to explain how they'd come to this point and why a Special Agent was helping them. In the end, she went with the truth. She felt full of surprises lately. Maybe it was the new hair.

Laurie was alive, but hanging on by a thread. She was the first person taken off the scene and the female State Police detective, Jill Freer, who was interrogating Carolina told her that medics suspected she had a skull fracture and a brain bleed. The odds seemed slim, but at least there was a chance.

Freer's partner, a stick up his ass type named Hallahan, stopped just short of cussing Carolina out for the plan she'd hatched up. She responded by actually cussing him out and reminding him that a variety of police departments had a chance to solve this and did nothing. He was on the verge of coming back at her before Freer shooed him aside.

When it was just the two of them, Freer let it be known that she didn't approve either. But, the woman, who was in her mid-forties with a haircut that would have looked just as good on a man as it did her, wasn't a complete prick.

As paramedics worked on Carolina's leg, Freer commented, "You're lucky you aren't dead."

"Tell me something I don't know," she said, watching the stretcher go by with Earl's body strapped to it. She glanced around, searching for Virginia, hoping she didn't have to see this. The woman was on the porch of the farmhouse, knees drawn to her chest, rocking back and forth.

"Do you have a social worker, or a psychologist? Someone who can talk to her?" Carolina motioned toward Virginia.

Freer nodded. "Yeah. She'll be here shortly."

"Good," Carolina said. "That woman saved me. Probably saved a lot of women."

Freer sat on the bumper of the ambulance, beside Carolina. "It wasn't just her, you know. You're the one that got this ball rolling. Maybe, no, definitely, not in the way I would have, but... I suppose it's all the same in the end."

Except for Jack, Carolina thought.

"If you say so."

"I do. You've got guts. Maybe not brains, but guts."

Carolina peered out across the landscape, upset, maybe broken, but relieved it was finally over.

"Thanks, I guess."

CHAPTER FIFTY-ONE

HER VAN WAS PACKED AND READY FOR THE ROAD. ALL that was left was the awkward goodbye. Five days had passed and Max had already returned to New York, vowing that he would not get involved the next time Carolina found herself in trouble. Carolina didn't believe him though. They made a pretty good pair, even if he was a blogger.

Scarlet sat on Carolina's mattress, visibly grossed out by her living situation but refraining from saying it aloud. She watched as Carolina put freshly laundered clothing into drawers. She had to rearrange some things because Scarlet had set her up with a custom makeup kit and a few other trinkets—earrings, bracelets, even an anklet that Carolina thought was a twisted joke. The gifts were appreciated, but Carolina imagined they'd end up in a pawn shop when the sentimentality wore off.

Still, whatever kept her sister happy was fine with her because Scarlet was starting to seem alive again. Her drinking was under control and she seemed as stable as could be expected, all things considered.

"You know, you could stay longer. I mean, if you wanted," Scarlet said.

Carolina smiled. "I appreciate that. But you don't need me cramping your style. I know I'm a lot to handle. And I'm sure your neighbors will be glad my van's out of their parking lot."

Scarlet laughed, a sound that was more common these days. And most welcome. "Are you going back to West Virginia?"

"For a little while. I'm sure Mom needs to yell at me. May as well let her get that out of her system. Then we'll see how it goes."

"Well, tell her I'll be down for a visit soon. And that I love her."

Carolina gave an exaggerated, sarcastic groan. "Oh, God, you two and the schmoopy shit. I can't even."

Scarlet smiled, but her eyes lost some of their humor. "You need to tolerate her, you know. She's not June Cleaver, but she cares."

Carolina noticed her sister's change in demeanor. She didn't mean to pry, but it came so naturally.

"What's with the sad puppy dog eyes?" she asked.

Scarlet shook her head, dismissive. "It's nothing."

"Bullshit. Tell me."

"Talking about Mom, it just made me think of Virginia Ripken. I mean, can you begin to imagine her life now? No husband, no money. Everyone knows her kid was some sick fuck serial killer that she had to shoot? I just... It would be too much, you know?"

Carolina grabbed her sister's hand, trying to comfort her. "No, I couldn't imagine," she said. "But sometimes life sucks like that."

"I've been thinking of going to visit her. Would that be weird?"

"Why?" Carolina asked.

"Why would it be weird?"

"No, why would you want to do that?"

"I don't know. To tell her I'm sorry for what she's going through. And to let her know that she's not alone in this world."

Carolina shook her head as she looked at her sister. She really was the tender-hearted one in the family. "You're too soft, sometimes. You know that?"

"And you're too hard," Scarlet said.

Carolina nodded. "We're like those bears in the Goldilocks story, except there's no middle ground."

"Maybe there doesn't need to be," Scarlet said as she rose from the mattress and moved to the sliding door. She dropped from the van, looking up at Carolina. "I can't thank you enough for what you did. I just want you to know that."

Carolina shrugged. She didn't feel like much of a hero. "I'll see you around sis." She slid into the driver's seat, shoved her key into the ignition.

"You never called me that before," Scarlet said.

"What?"

"Sis?"

Carolina gunned the engine. "Oh. Well, don't get used to it."

Scarlet grinned as she slid the door closed and, with that, Carolina was back on the road.

CHAPTER FIFTY-TWO

Carolina watched Pittsburgh fade away in her rearview mirror. She felt good, leaving it behind her. Something about being in Dupray, that boring, mundane, small town, seemed to call to her.

Not that she would admit to anyone.

As much as she protested, as much as she mocked it, as her GPS counted down the miles to Dupray, West Virginia, she felt a sense of calm wash over her.

She felt like she was going home.

CHAPTER FIFTY-THREE

SCARLET SAT OUTSIDE VIRGINIA RIPKEN'S HOUSE FOR almost half an hour before working up the nerve to exit her Mercedes SUV and walk to the front door. She almost left a half dozen times, but her conscience kept telling her this was the right thing to do. That being kind was always the best option.

She pulled the screen door open, tapping the interior door with her knuckles. Inside she could hear the familiar clatter of pots and pans. She must be making lunch, Scarlet thought, and almost fled, not wanting to intrude.

Instead, she knocked again, harder. The door wasn't latched and eased open an inch.

"Virginia?" Scarlet called through the opening.

She waited, heard approaching footsteps then a woman's tentative voice.

"Who's out there?" Virginia asked.

"It's Scarlet. Scarlet Engle."

The door whipped open and she saw the woman she had met less than a week before. She looked like death. Gone was the cherubic smiling, sweet older lady. Now Virginia looked barren and broken. Like a woman with nothing left and no reason to go on.

Scarlet's heart broke for her.

"I'm sorry to bother you," Scarlet said. "Maybe I shouldn't have come, but I just needed to say thank you."

Virginia Ripken only stared, her face as blank as a mannequin.

"I'm sorry," Scarlet repeated, feeling like that old saying about best intentions was living out right before her eyes. "You're busy and I shouldn't have bothered you."

She spun away, hurrying up the overgrown walk, when Virginia finally responded.

"Scarlet. I'm sorry. I just haven't been myself lately. Please, do come in."

When Scarlet turned back she found the woman crying.

"Maybe you're psychic, because I could really use the company," Virginia said, offering a broken smile.

Scarlet nodded and returned, stepping through the door as Virginia held it open for her.

Inside, the house was a mess with boxes piled everywhere. All were labeled. Kitchen. Living Room. Knick knacks. Glassware.

"Are you moving?"

Virginia nodded. "I am. I can't even walk out of my house without the neighbors staring. Reporters keep showing up all hours of the day. That's why I didn't answer at first when you knocked. A trip to the corner market is enough to gather a crowd. I feel like a lion in a zoo. I just can't take it."

"I'm so sorry to hear that," Scarlet said, adding *Her Home* to the long list of things this poor woman had lost.

Virginia waved her hand. "Such is life. No one promised it would be easy."

They stood in awkward silence for a long moment, then

Virginia motioned to a card table set up in the kitchen. "Please have a seat. I'm sorry the good furniture's already in storage."

"I don't mind at all," Scarlet said, dropping onto a folding lawn chair. "How are you managing?" she asked, hopeful it wouldn't be viewed as intrusive.

Virginia grabbed a coffee pot from the counter and refilled her cup. Even though it was steaming, she took a long swallow.

"I haven't gotten more than five hours sleep combined since... well, you know. I swear coffee's the only thing that keeps me moving."

Scarlet reached out and took Virginia's free hand, trying to comfort the woman.

"I understand," Scarlet said. "I'm the same way. I'm useless without my java."

Virginia looked up and met Scarlet with a weak smile. She reached into a nearby box marked Dishes & Glasses and extracted a cup, sliding it to Scarlet.

"Help yourself," she said.

Scarlet did. It wasn't Starbucks, but the brew would suffice. Besides, she was there to commiserate, not freeload.

Virginia let out an exhausted breath. "I really do appreciate you coming by. I've been so lonely. It's nice to have some company."

The last vestiges of guilt and worry that Scarlet felt for intruding drifted away. She'd done the right thing after all and maybe, together, they could find a way to heal their lingering wounds.

CHAPTER FIFTY-FOUR

"Y'ellow," Elven said, his voice crackling across the cell phone connection.

"How's sheriffing going these days?" Carolina asked, a smile creeping onto her face.

"Well hello there to you too, Carolina. I assumed you'd forgotten all about me now that you're a big city gal." He added extra twang to his voice when he said it.

"To forget about someone would mean that I gave a shit about them in the first place," Carolina retorted.

"Words hurt," he said, stifling a laugh.

"Anything new in West Virginia's sleepiest town?"

"Plenty," he said. "But most are too sensitive to discuss over the phone. Do remind me though to tell you about Buster Smithy and the stolen bighorn sheep."

"Sounds fucking fascinating," Carolina said.

"You jest," Elven said. "Although, I imagine our small town adventures pale in comparison to your recent endeavors. I spoke with Beatrice the other day and she gave me the scoop."

"Did she?" Carolina said. "We purposely left her out of the

loop on much of it. Some things a mother doesn't need to know."

"I had a feeling that might be the case. So, I gave Terrell Werner a call to find out the rest. And to make sure you behaved and didn't tarnish my sterling reputation."

Carolina's smile grew wider. She was glad they were talking on the phone, though, because she begrudged him the satisfaction of knowing she enjoyed these chats. "I don't think he likes me much," Carolina said.

"Oh, no thinking required. The man abhors your presence. I believe his exact words were, 'Keep her in West Virginia from now on.' He may have sprinkled in some profanities too. Words that don't cross my tongue as you well know." His grin came through in his voice.

"And what did you say?"

"I told him you're a free bird, and this bird you cannot change."

She lost it, unable to hold back a laugh. "Very poetic. Maybe you need to change your name to Sheriff Skynyrd. Has a good ring to it."

"That it does," Elven said. Then his voice turned more serious. "How are you though, Carolina. Sounds like you went through quite a bad spell."

Understatement of the century, Carolina thought. "I'm here. And there's one less evil motherfucker in the world. I'm calling it a win."

"That boy did sound like a special sort of crazy. Surprised me though, how he could manage to use those phone apps and send text messages when, the way Terrell told me, he was next thing to a simpleton."

Carolina's smile faded as she thought about Earl and his games. His childlike yet viscous personality.

"What do I know, though," he said. "I'm just a small town Sheriff running down stolen sheep."

"Don't sell yourself short, Elven," she said. But she didn't want to get lost in recent events. Her journey had barely begun. She still had a few hundred miles to go, and she didn't want to spend them rehashing all her mistakes.

"From the sounds of it, you're driving. Are you coming back to Dupray? Dare I ask?"

"You just did," Carolina said. "And I am. How is Bea, anyway?"

"Seems like a question you should ask yourself rather than through an intermediary."

"Easier said than done. You know how she is."

"I know your half of the story," Elven said. "Quite the odd relationship you two have. You won't ask her the price of tea in China but when she asks you to put your life on hold and drive to Pittsburgh to play undercover cop, you jump." He clucked his tongue. "As I said, odd."

"You have a mother, you should know how it works. Kids will do anything for dear old mom. Always trying to win that affection."

"So you say. Beatrice is fine, and that's all I'm offering. Try talking to her when you get back in town. Just be a daughter for once, not a hero."

Carolina fell silent, thinking about the words she'd spoken. *Kids will do anything for dear old mom.*

"Carolina? You there?" Elven asked. "Did I lose you?"

"Oh, fuck," Carolina said.

"What's the matter?"

"Sorry, Elven, I gotta go." Carolina ended the call.

How the hell had she missed it? But she knew why. Because the drugs, the withdrawal, had slowed her wits and clouded her mind, but not in the way she wanted.

She dialed Max and he picked up on the second ring. Before he could say a word, she was already talking.

"Give me Virginia's address," Carolina said.

"What? Why??"

"Just do it Max!"

"Uh, something with a tree. Sycamore or some shit," Max said. "Why?"

"I need the exact address. Right now!"

Ahead she saw a turnaround on the interstate, the type meant only for use by emergency vehicles. She whipped a U-turn and could hear Max typing in the background. Flooring the gas pedal, the van launching into its top speed of seventy miles per hour, she waited, impatient.

"Come on, Ma—"

"It's nineteen fifty-three Sequoia Lane, Sallow Creek, PA. Now what—"

She cut him off, punching the address into her GPS. She was closer than she thought, less than ten miles out. But she might already be too late.

CHAPTER FIFTY-FIVE

SCARLET HAD LEFT HER CELL IN HER CAR SO SHE DIDN'T hear her phone blow up with texts and calls from Carolina. Instead she and Virginia Ripken drowned their sorrows in day reheated, old coffee and reflected upon their shared trauma.

"How are you holding up, though?" Scarlet asked.

Virginia shrugged. "Not well. But I'm sure you could tell that the moment you saw me at the door," Virginia said. "I must look like a used dishrag. Especially to someone so perfect and pretty as you."

Scarlet gave a shy smile. "I'm just good with a makeup brush is all."

"My Reggie liked women who wore makeup," Virginia said. "I tried once, for him, but I ended up looking more like Bozo the Clown than Cindy Crawford. Guess I'm not built for it."

"It just takes practice," Scarlet said. "Carolina's the same way. She doesn't know the difference between a stippling and a contour brush."

"That's all over my head." Virginia held up her hands, submissive. "My Reggie, he would have loved you though."

Scarlet shifted her eyes to her cup, hoping the awkward moment would pass.

"You were just his type, you know," Virginia said, looking straight at Scarlet. "He always liked the sluts."

Scarlet's eyes snapped to Virginia's face. "I'm sorry, what?" she asked, unsure if she heard correctly. But there it was, on Virginia's face. A smile that was almost malicious.

"Blonde, big boobs. Legs wiiiiide open for anyone with a fat wallet," Virginia said.

Scarlet rose quickly, sending her chair skittering across the tile floor. "I'm sorry I bothered you." She hurried to the exit.

"Sure, go," Virginia said, waving one hand and finishing her coffee with the other. "Just run away. You don't care that my husband's dead. That I can't collect my own newspaper from the driveway without the neighbors gawking. That I had to kill my own son because of some dirty whores. But you just go ahead. Leave."

Her words dripped with venom. Scarlet didn't need or want to say anything else. She continued scurrying, desperate to get away from the woman. She heard Virginia's feet as she followed.

"My life is ruined because of you and your slut friends. My Reggie, he spent our life's savings on dirty whores."

Scarlet picked up the pace but in her rush, her foot caught on one of the boxes and she stumbled sideways. A tower of cardboard toppled, careening into the wall, objects inside breaking.

"But I showed him!" Virginia said. "My Earl, he never loved his daddy the way he did me. So he took care of Reggie for me."

As she regained her balance, Scarlet turned and saw Virginia make a swinging motion with her arms.

"He never saw it coming," Virginia said. "The scythe, Earl always kept it good and sharp. And the hogs took care of the rest."

Scarlet jerked the door open and sprinted down the steps. Virginia chased after her.

"It was so easy catching you and your slut friends," Virginia continued. "Just flash a few hundred dollar bills and you'd show up wherever I told you to go. No questions asked. I suppose Reginald was good for something. If it wasn't for that filthy phone app, I wouldn't have known where to start."

The woman was screaming, irate, foaming at the mouth. And cackling like a maniac.

CHAPTER FIFTY-SIX

THE BRAKES SHRIEKED AS CAROLINA SKIDDED TO A STOP IN front of Virginia Ripken's house. Scarlet was running through the lawn, toward her SUV, and the old woman chased after, her gray hair flopping wildly behind her and looking like a suburban witch who'd lost her broom.

Carolina jumped out of the van, the engine still running, and Scarlet saw her.

"She's fucking crazy!" She pointed to Virginia who stood on her lawn, glaring at them.

"Get over here," Carolina said, pushing her sister toward the relative safety of the van and putting herself between her sister and her would-be attacker.

Carolina strode toward Virginia. "You thought you were so clever, but I know you're the one who sent the texts. Who chose and lured in the women." She reached for her gun, leveling it at Virginia to hold her at bay.

"I see where all the brains went in the family," Virginia said, her face twisting into a grimace. "Such a shame it took you so long though."

"The cops are already on their way. And you'll get to spend however many miserable years you have left locked in a cage. I just wish there was someone who could torture you the way your fucked up son tormented those women."

Virginia only laughed.

Carolina took a step closer, trying to verify if what she thought she saw was real. It was. Foamy, blood-tinged saliva oozed from the woman's mouth. It ran down her cheeks, dripped onto her clothes. Faster it came, mouthfuls of it.

Virginia began to cough and retch. She fell to her knees, dropping into the overgrown grass. Her body shook and spasmed. Her hands dug at her stomach, tearing through her own shirt.

Then all movement stopped.

Sirens wailed in the background. The police were close.

Carolina moved closer, needing to verify that she was in fact, dead. She used her foot to shake Virginia's upper body. The woman's head lolled to the side, blood draining from her gaping maw.

"What the hell was that?" Carolina asked, turning to her sister.

Scarlet sucked in labored breaths. "I don't know. She was nice, but then just flipped like a switch. She was screaming at me about everything. Calling me names. Telling me that she had Earl kill her husband and—"

Scarlet froze, her face contorting in pain. She doubled over, holding her midsection.

"What's the matter?" Carolina asked.

"I don't know, I feel s—" Scarlet gagged, upchucked a mouthful of blood.

She staggered, almost falling. Carolina got her arm around her back just in time, holding her steady as two police cars pulled onto the scene.

"Get over here!" Carolina screamed. "My sister's dying!"

CHAPTER FIFTY-SEVEN

Carolina sat in a chair next to Scarlet's hospital bed. Monitors beeped in a soothing rhythm, one that threatened to lull her to sleep, to join her sister and finally get some rest. She shifted in the chair, trying to fight off a nap that so desperately wanted to come.

Scarlet's eyelids fluttered, opened. Black stains lingered around her mouth from the activated charcoal the paramedics had applied. The act that saved her life. Now that Scarlet was going to be fine, Carolina was tempted to snap a photo of her disheveled face. Something she could use as blackmail material for the rest of their lives.

"Where am I?" Scarlet asked.

Carolina scooted her chair closer to the bed. "I thought that was obvious. You're in the hospital."

"What happened?" Scarlet asked, still drowsy.

"You should have passed on the coffee," Carolina said. "It was full of gopher poison. Strychnine."

"No wonder it tasted like shit." She smiled and despite it all looked beautiful. The bitch. "What about Virginia?" Scarlet asked.

"Apparently she didn't want to go on living without dear, dead, deranged Earl so she mixed herself up a triple death latte to do the job. Then you showed up and I guess she figured, two birds, one stone..."

Always with the birds.

"Did they save her too?" Scarlet asked.

"No. She hemorrhaged on the lawn. They didn't even try."

"Good," Scarlet said, closing her eyes again. "I'm glad."

"Finally, something we both can agree on," Carolina said, slouching in the chair and closing her own eyes.

She'd earned a few z's.

FROM THE AUTHORS

Thank you for reading book 3 in Carolina's adventures! We hope you enjoyed it. Book 4 is nearing completion and you can preorder Poaching Grounds now and have it ready on release day.

As authors without million dollar ad budgets, reviews are very important to both the success of the book and our careers so, if you enjoyed the book, please consider a quick jaunt to Amazon or Goodreads to share your thoughts.

Again please accept our most sincere thanks & happy reading!

-Tony

-Drew

Join Drew's mailing list - http://drewstricklandbooks.com/readers-list

Join Tony's mailing list - http://tonyurbanauthor.com/signup

MORE FROM TONY & DREW

Hell on Earth
Within the Woods
Soulless Wanderer
Patriarch
A Land Darkened

Made in United States
Orlando, FL
27 May 2024